Law of the Jungle

A novella

by

CHRISTINA HOAG

Better Than Starbucks
Publications

Law of the Jungle

First Printing: ISBN 978-1-7376219-1-1

Cover by Better Than Starbucks

Better Than Starbucks Publications
P.O.Box 673, Mayo, FL 32066

If you prick us, do we not bleed? If you tickle us, do we not laugh? If you poison us, do we not die? And if you wrong us, shall we not revenge?

— William Shakespeare, *The Merchant of Venice*

PART I

My ears detected them well before my eyes, which is frequently the case in the jungle. When you're used to living solely with parrot chatter and monkey howls, interlopers walking in the forest sound like a stampede of elephants. Judging by the boot thuds, the crackling of broken brush, a number of people were coming my way. Narcotraffickers? Arms smugglers? Guerrillas, illegal miners, loggers, other lawless purveyors of various contraband that plied the Amazon basin? This didn't bode well. Not well at all.

I got up from my desk, where I'd been updating my research notes. I turned to see a herd of National Guard soldiers entering the camp clearing. Clad in fatigues, assault rifles slung across the front of their torsos, ready to be picked up and pointed. At me, evidently.

The head elephant stepped forward.

"Doctora Rowena Aldus, your permit is under review by the National Institute for Scientific Research. You must come with us."

My stomach plummeted. Carlota, my solicitor in the nearest town of San Carlos de Rio Negro and only friend in the world, had warned me months ago that this would happen sooner or later. The Venezuelan government was evaluating all foreign projects to determine if they met the national socialist mission. If not, I'd be "invited to leave." I'd laughed it off. I'd been in the jungle for seventeen years researching the priapic properties of the venom of the phoneutria fera, known more colloquially as the Brazilian wandering spider, as a possible erectile dysfunction drug. I was a harmless fixture, that daft inglesa the locals humored and chuckled at behind my back. The government wouldn't give me the heave-ho.

Or would they? I counted nine men. La guardia had certainly gone to a great deal of effort to bring me in, indicating this was perhaps more serious than I'd reckoned.

"These orders come from Caracas, Doctora. I would advise you that it's in your best interest to accompany us." The guardsman exhibited the usual officiousness of minions who, granted even a modicum of power, got carried away with it.

"Would you grant me the favor of five minutes to arrange a few things for the trip?" I employed the obsequious language and deferential tone that local officialdom expected as a sign of respect.

He puffed his chest slightly and nodded, then directed his men to fan out around the camp, I suppose to prevent me from scarpering into the forest because I was such a dangerous criminal.

I inserted my field notes into a plastic bag and went to one of my four mud-brick huts encircling the clearing. After removing my stainless-steel lockbox from its cubby-hole between the walls and the palm-thatch roof, I placed the bag with my notes inside and drew out a bag containing my passport, research permit and various other items of importance, including my degree from Oxford and the handful of photographs I had of my late father. I debated whether to take the photos and my academic credentials, but then I reasoned that even if they were to chuck me out of the country, I'd surely be allowed one more trip to collect my personal belongings. I took out my passport and permit and left the rest in the box, which I wedged back into its spot.

As we tramped down the path to the boat landing on the riverbank, children from the neighboring village, who'd obviously been in the bush observing the goings-on, scampered ahead. When we arrived at the settlement five minutes later, the women had come out of their huts to watch me being rather unceremoniously escorted to the waiting boats. The men were probably gone hunting. I called to the children in Nheengatu, trying to gloss over the import of the scene.

"Feed my spiders and I'll bring you back lots of goodies from town!"

They all smiled. I gave them sweets and small toys in return for catching the mice, small lizards and insects that formed the phoneutria fera's diet, but whether they'd do it if my absence stretched beyond a day or two, I didn't know. I'd never been gone long from camp.

I clambered into one of the Guardia Nacional's two boats, emblazoned with red stripes, and was handed a life jacket. As engines spluttered to life, we zoomed off. I gave a jaunty wave, belying the unease that was pinching me, as the villagers lined the shore with solemn faces. We skidded around a bend in the tributary and then entered the main waterway.

Carlota was waiting for me at the Guardia station in San Carlos when we arrived after the two-plus hour journey, which I usually found meditative, but this time found achingly slow. I was anxious to get this resolved as quickly as possible. She clutched a dirty canvas bag under an arm, which I suspected had something to do with my plight as I'd never seen her with such a filthy accessory. She was a natty dresser for these parts.

She pulled me into her shroud of perfume and kissed my cheek in the Venezuelan custom. It felt a bit awkward, as always, but not altogether disagreeable. I'd grown used to the lack of human physical contact well before my solitary life in the jungle. My father was the only person to have ever shown me real affection.

"I heard la guardia was bringing you in today and I spoke to the comandante," Carlota said. News spread quickly in town. At one thousand two hundred inhabitants, it was actually smaller than the grammar school I'd attended in Cornwall. "You're going to have to report to the Institute in Puerto Ayacucho. There's a flight leaving in forty minutes."

"I can't deal with this from here?" I was filled with dread. The capital of Amazonas State to the north was a rambunctious, dirty place, full of cars and crowds.

"El comandante said the order came from the Interior Ministry in Caracas. Nothing he can do. I did tell you this was serious."

"I haven't even brought anything for a trip."

Carlota pulled the canvas bag off her shoulder and offered it to me. "I thought so. You'll need this then. I should warn you. There's not much left in your account."

I peeked inside the bag. It contained bundles of grubby looking notes. Bleakly, I stuffed it into my rucksack. Thanks to Venezuela's perpetually devaluing currency, it was quite a pile, but the bag itself was probably worth more than all the bolívars.

The inheritance from my parents was indeed dwindling, but what was I to do? Several big drug companies had financed me in my early years, but after the initial tranche of funds, they hadn't renewed. When I inquired about the reasons, I discovered that the corporate white coats they'd sent were in fact turncoats. They'd reported me, in varying terms, as "difficult to work with," "addled by the tropics" and "unlikely to ever finish." Science was not about money, I fired back in emails to the heads of R&D. "It's about precision and accuracy." They did not reply.

"Doctora!" Unsure of whom he was addressing, since female lawyers are also called "doctora" in Venezuela, we both swiveled to see a wiry man in fatigues approaching. I recognized the comandante, who was charged with law and order in southern Amazonas.

"We must get to the airport," he said. "I ordered them to hold the plane for you."

I plastered on a specious smile that disguised my growing nerves. "Ready when you are, Comandante."

Nine days later, things were not going quite as swimmingly as I'd hoped. Despite the urgency of whisking me off to Puerto Ayacucho, I still had not been granted an audience with the person who held my fate in her hands — the Institute of Scientific Research's Amazonas director, Doctora (How Venezuelans love their honorifics!) Yesenia Olivia Ulloa, to whom I privately referred by her acronymic initials YOU. YOU was invariably engaged although the busiest person I'd seen in the building was the middle-aged maid, who ferried trays upon trays of thimble-sized coffees to various offices. I supposed their invisible denizens were in dire need of pick-me-ups to cope with their long hours of strenuous toil.

I'd taken to spending my days staking out the building's foyer in hopes of catching YOU on the in or the out, but I'd not so much as caught a glimpse. Did YOU actually exist? One day I spent three and a half hours sitting on a toilet in the ladies, thinking I could surely ambush her at the sink. But despite imbibing all that coffee, YOU must've had a super-human bladder. The only person who entered was the maid. After finding me there three times, she reported me to the receptionist, Clodosvaldo, who'd knocked on the door and told me I had to vacate forthwith. Since then, I'd assisted Clodo with his crossword clues, although he actually was quite adept. He got plenty of practice.

I was well used to the blurry notion of time in the tropics. For example, the Spanish word for now, "ahora," could mean any time that day. Still, I was getting impatient. I doubted the tribe would've fed my spiders during this lengthy absence. They were afraid of them. Then there was the camp itself. It wouldn't take long before scavengers descended once it got around that I was gone. The other threat was the jungle itself, which grew over vestiges of human inhabitation with remarkable celerity. And all the while, of course, my pile of bank notes was shrinking with my purchases of clothing, toiletries, food, and lodging.

I was perusing the local newspaper in the Institute foyer one morning, something I liked to do whenever I arrived in civilization to catch up with the world-at-large, when I heard my name pronounced in a gringo accent. I flicked down a top corner of the newspaper page. A tall man stared at me from across the room, fair-haired, his face flushed and dewed with perspiration. A representative from a pharmaceutical company? Although, outfitted in a garish orange and black Hawaiian shirt and Panama hat, he didn't look like one. Scientist types usually arrived in brand new khaki outfits ordered from safari catalogues.

"And you are?" I put on my best haughty voice.

"It's incredible running into you like this. It saved me a full-on expedition into the jungle," he said in a tumble of words. An American. He possessed a disarming smile complemented by a set of even, gleaming, very American teeth. He extended a hand. "Guy Westerphal."

I gave his clammy palm a brief, tepid shake. He gestured at the seat next to me. "May I?"

I cocked my head, feigning indifference.

Guy sat, mopped his face with a handkerchief and stuffed it into his breast pocket like a magician shoving a silk hanky into a wand that would miraculously turn it into a rose. "I've been looking for you for some time. Your biochemistry professor at Oxford, Dr. Medford-Jones, told me you were in the Venezuelan Amazon. I figured someone here at the Institute would know your exact coordinates if you were still around."

The name jolted me. The last time I'd been in contact with Rupert was shortly after I arrived in Venezuela following completion of my doctorate.

"You certainly took a chance that I was still here," I said.

"I like risks." He grinned, rather cheekily I thought. "I tried to get information about you from the Institute over the phone, but they weren't very forthcoming. A Venezuelan friend told me I'd likely get further in person and by offering a 'donation'." He hooked his fingers in the air. Did he mean quotation marks? A peculiar gesture. "I thought, 'What the hell? I'll go down there myself. I like road trips.' I got in yesterday and came right over. The guy," he hooked a thumb in Clodo's direction, "told me you'd likely be here this morning."

I glanced at Clodo. I'd thought we were on friendly enough terms that he would've told me first thing that a foreigner had come looking for me, especially after all the puzzle clues I'd helped him with, but of course, that was people for you. Feckless. I turned back to Guy. There had to be opportunity in this act of providence. I couldn't appear as desperate as I was. I drew myself up.

"I have an important appointment with the Institute director in a few minutes, Mr. Westerphal."

"Guy, please. I'd like to talk to you about your research project. I have a business plan that may interest you."

The exit sign above the closed door of my predicament suddenly illuminated. I couldn't contain myself. "Perhaps we should talk about this in a more private setting." I stood.

"What about your appointment?"

I waved a hand airily. "I'll reschedule."

We headed outside. As I passed Clodo, I noticed that his shirt looked new. My presence had probably bought him a whole new wardrobe.

Trusting that Guy would foot the bill, I steered him to the nicest restaurant in town where we sat on the terrace. Two small monkeys frolicked along the railing, stopping in front of us for a handout.

"Aren't they cute?" Guy said with tourist delight.

"They're capuchins, clever little things. Probably the restaurant's pets. People often keep monkeys here."

After ordering overpriced, over sugared watermelon juice for us, I leaned back in a cushioned wicker chair and casually bobbed a crossed leg, affecting a nonchalant air.

"You're probably wondering how I learned about you," Guy began over the faint roar of the blender as our juices were being made.

"I admit it had crossed my mind."

He fanned himself with the menu. "I read an article you wrote in the Journal of Natural Chemistry about how the phoneutria fera's bite causes long-lasting erections in men and the tremendous potential of this property in the venom."

My leg stopped bobbing. "That was quite a few years ago."

"It was, but it caught my attention. The fact is, I've been looking for a new business to invest in and I remembered that article. I did some checking around and found that despite trying, no one has made this venom work. Your name kept cropping up as I did my due diligence, but I couldn't locate you. I tried the journal, Oxford, and of course the internet, but everything was a dead end, so I put it aside.

"Then over a year later, I came across an article about Professor Medford-Jones retiring, and he mentioned some of his students and their research areas over the years, including one who was studying the Brazilian wandering spider in the Venezuelan Amazon. I thought this could be the author of that article, so I called Oxford and got an email address for Medford. He confirmed he was referring to Rowena Aldus and suggested starting my search with the Institute in Puerto Ayacucho since they kept tabs on all scientific research in the Amazon. He said he'd often wondered what had happened to you over the years."

Guy seemed like a forty-year-old Boy Scout enthused by discovering animal spoor in the woods. I couldn't help but admire his persistence, as well as feel flattered by it. I lowered my customary shield just a tad.

"You're quite the sleuth," I said.

Our frothy crimson drinks arrived in tall tumblers neatly wrapped in cloth napkins so our fingers wouldn't slip on the sweating glass. Guy downed his in gulps.

"Otro por favor," he said in a loud voice and cringeworthy accent. "Love these fresh fruit juices." He leaned forward, arms on his knees. "I'm going to get right to the point. I'm intrigued by the venom's properties as they relate to ED. Now I know what you're going to say: there are already a number of those pharmaceuticals on the market, but," he held up a finger, "they're only available via prescription and insurers will only pay for them if ED is diagnosed. That leaves a lot of consumers who want ED drugs but can't afford to buy them or get a prescription. If we were to make a pill from a natural source, it could be marketed as a supplement. That means it wouldn't have to go through FDA approval. The Food and Drug Administration," he added.

I nodded impatiently, eager to hear the rest.

"As I'm sure you know, it takes years, trials upon trials, to get a drug approved in the U.S. But with a supplement, we'd be able to do a quick turnaround to product launch. We could then market the supplement at a lower price point, go for volume to establish the market, then gradually raise the price. We'd maintain complete control over the patent, and that's key. A pharmaceutical only has patent protection for ten years. Then anybody can copy it, including the Chinese."

His words were a torrent of business jargon. "You certainly have it well thought out" was my rather feeble response.

"I wouldn't be here if I didn't think it could work. Listen, I've heard you've walked away from the Big Pharma boys in the past, but those companies aren't me."

He'd certainly done his homework. He grinned again, exuding that Yankee confidence born of New World optimism. Some would classify it as bravado and others as naïveté. However you saw it, it had certainly got them quite far.

"Well, you're an . . . entrepreneur." My rejoinder was admittedly lame.

"I prefer the term 'angel investor.' Make no mistake, I'm in it to make money, just like Big Pharma's all about profits too, but I don't have a stable of projects competing against each other to be the next blockbuster drug, corporate overhead to pay, shareholders to answer to. It's just me so I can move as fast or as slowly as I want. I propose a fifty-fifty partnership. You'd have free rein over the science. I'd be in charge of business."

I blinked, stunned. None of the pharma companies had ever come close to proposing a deal along these lines or used the word partnership.

Guy sat back, gripping the chair arms. "I just can't get over bumping into you like this. It seems like it was meant to be."

"Yes, it's extraordinary you caught me in Puerto Ayacucho," I said amidst my daze. "I rarely come here."

"I was ready to head downriver in a dugout canoe if I had to."

"Well, luckily, you didn't have to." I pressed my lips into a magnanimous smile.

The waiter delivered Guy's second juice, and Guy asked me whether I'd like another one or something to eat. I shook my head. It struck me that I was at a disadvantage. I'd spent far too much time alone over the years, and my social skills, admittedly never nimble to begin with, lagged substantially. Holding a complex conversation, moreover in English which I rarely spoke, was like levering rusty cogs into motion.

"I really must be off actually. I'll have a think about your proposition."

"Your consideration is all I can ask. I know it must be a shock, a random stranger parachuting in on you like this. What about discussing everything over dinner tonight?"

I wasn't going to turn down a free meal. Since my arrival, my diet had consisted largely of rice and black beans to stretch my limited funds. "I believe I'm free."

He handed me a business card and we arranged to meet at the restaurant of his hotel. As I strolled off, something expanded inside me to the point of bursting. I have to admit, Guy's enthusiasm was infectious. I hadn't felt such . . . excitement, I supposed it was, since I was a child when my father's eyes would light up at a nest of robin's eggs we'd stumbled upon or spring shoots on jonquil bulbs we'd planted. "Now we'll see what happens next!" he'd say.

I reined myself in. First, I had to vet this man. I turned into an internet café and paid for an hour of time. I sat at a computer, took out his card from my pocket and studied it. It simply had his name with "Venture capitalist & start-up consultant" in elegant cursive underneath. It listed a phone number and email address. That was the extent of it. I liked that it wasn't fussy and overdone. I set it down and typed "Guy Westerphal" into the search field.

A profile on a website called BusinessLink popped up. It listed his current employment as stated on the business card and gave the additional detail that it was located in Miami, which made sense since it served as Latin America's de facto business capital. His past employment was a string of private equity firms, hedge funds, and investment banks. He'd certainly hopped around a lot. He held an MBA from the Wharton School of Business, University of Pennsylvania. His bonafides as a businessman checked out and then some.

I stared at the thumbnail photo of Guy on the screen. He bore a resemblance to my father. Dad's hair had been pale ginger whisps parted on the side. Guy was blonde, but his hair was also fine and side parted. Dad had a long, straight nose, Guy's was straight but blunter. They both had blue eyes, Dad's darker like lapis lazuli whilst Guy's were lighter, glacier blue. I stirred myself and returned to the search results. That seemed to be the only item for "Guy Westerphal."

Since I had time to spare, I typed in "Adelaide Aldus death Cornwall UK." No harm in checking on my dear late mother whilst I was at it.

No results found. Good.

I strolled back to my grotty digs, the cheapest hotel in town, located next to the market. The refuse pile of rotting fruit and vegetables gave off a ferocious stench that, sadly, I had got accustomed to, as had the pickers who swarmed over it at day's end hunting for passable produce to eat or sell.

The cacophony of sound, however, I could never get used to. Men, standing in the beds of pickup trucks, shouted as they threw down baskets of papayas, bananas, and guavas to waiting helpers. Women clapped and whistled to sell their wares, from dish towels to aluminum pots. Bus engines snorted. Car horns blared.

That day I neither smelt nor heard any of it. My mind was on the surprise of Guy and his proposal. As I sank onto the edge of the cratered mattress in my cement cell of a room, I felt exhausted from dealing with everything myself all the time. The National Guard, money worries, bureaucratic tangles. I had Carlota, of course, but it would be a relief to have someone waving a magic wand who could take care of everything. I just wanted to do my research without bother. Guy's partnership looked to be just what I needed, but I had one condition that he might not like.

I had to calm down, not get ahead of myself. I took out one of the coloring books that I'd purchased and a box of crayons and began to shade a picture of a teddy bear with fuschia and orange stripes. My simple way of coping with stress. Gradually, my mind emptied, and my worries dissolved.

When I entered the restaurant that evening, I spotted him waving wildly at me. Feeling a prickle of embarrassment at his zeal, I glanced around to see if anyone was watching. It didn't seem like it. As I arrived at the table, he jumped up and pulled out my chair. Pushing it in, he leaned into the crook of my neck.

"What's that perfume you're wearing? It's divine."

I murmured something about a friend lending it to me. A mild embellishment. The wife of the couple who owned the hotel had undertaken my makeover with relish when I told her I was meeting a man for dinner. Over my protests that it was just a business affair, she painted me with makeup and lent me a short black skirt and tight purple top. Shoes, though, presented a problem. My feet were far too big to borrow her dressy sandals, so I'd worn my flip-flops, which I thought a better option than my sturdy jungle boots. Besides, my feet would be under a table. On my way out the door, she spritzed me with perfume and assured me I looked "bella." I took her word for it.

When I studied myself in a mirror in the hotel hallway, I saw a forty-two-year-old woman, with short, mannish-cut dark red hair framing a face which showed signs of too many years in a harsh climate that my genes hadn't prepared me for. Deep crow's feet at the corners of my eyes, lines across my forehead and cheeks, a jowl line that had begun to sag. For the first time in years, I wondered how other people viewed me. How did Guy see me? I dismissed the thought as frivolous. This was business, although with Guy's show of old-fashioned gallantry at the start, the evening seemed to be taking on a rather more personal note.

The waiter lit a white candle on the table then ambled off to fulfill Guy's order of a bottle of rosé, a luxury few in Venezuela could afford. "All right with you?" he said.

I'd sworn off booze since pub nights in my first year at Oxford had led me to my one and only disastrous adventure with a member of the opposite sex, but I didn't want Guy to think I was a spoilsport. "My favorite," I said firmly.

"I've always been an Anglophile. I just love Brits and your sense of humor. 'Fawlty Towers' and all that. And London's my favorite city in the world."

As far as I was concerned, London was nothing but people, pollution, and pricey everything. The only good bit was Paddington Station, where I caught the train to Oxford. But I made an effort to be amiable. "Lots of history," I said vaguely.

The wine arrived and Guy insisted on toasting. "To . . . well, to us, if I may be so bold." I clinked his glass and took a rather too grateful gulp. The rosé burned like a fuse down my gullet and landed with a rocky splash. Then the familiar tentacles of warmth undulated through me.

"So," he settled back in his chair, twirling the wineglass by its stem, "before we get to business, tell me everything about yourself."

The rosé in his glass cast a translucent glow in the candlelight. In that moment, I thought it was the most beautiful thing I'd ever seen, as magnificent as a maharajah's jewel. I looked up at him. He was gazing at me with the subtlest of smiles, waiting for me to speak. No one, I realized, had ever asked me to tell them more about myself than the perfunctory details of where I was from, university studies and the like, not even the R&D people who'd coveted my research. I had to drag through the sludge of my memory for the past that I'd buried. I always found it uncomfortable, revealing myself.

"I'm from southwest England, Cornwall. My father ran an antique book and stamp shop in a small inland town, which had a bit of a tourist trade in the summer months. He and my mother didn't get on, so ever since I can remember, he would take me, the only child, out on the moors, the cliffs, or the beach every chance he got. He was something of a naturalist. We'd tramp for hours, collect bits and bobs — feathers, the occasional fossil or artifact — visit historical sites and so forth. He taught me about botany and fauna. My mother was a herbalist, but her love of outdoors was limited to pottering around in her garden of medicinal plants. She sold salves and tinctures, that sort of thing, and built quite a robust following. When I was twelve, my father died. My mother sold all of Dad's books and stamps and moved her medicine business into the shop. Whenever I wasn't at school, I was working there. Luckily, I was able to escape through academics, to Oxford. She died shortly before I left for South America."

I stopped, startled by how much I'd said. The wine was having a disinhibiting effect. After getting over the initial pique of discomfort at talking about myself, I had to admit having someone interested in me wasn't altogether unpleasant. Guy topped up my glass.

"You're quite alone in the world, then."

"Yes, I suppose I am."

"And your interest in arachnids? Was it from your father or mother or neither?"

I was on a roll now. "My father respected all living things, even the ones that no one likes, including spiders and insects. He was fascinated by how animals adapt their physiology to their environments, so I suppose I inherited that. I became interested in tropical environments and biochemistry at Oxford. I travelled quite a lot throughout the Amazon basin for my studies."

"The 'savage murderess', though," Guy said. "An interesting choice of subject."

My eyes focused on him with the razor-sharp lens of sudden wariness. What did he know about why I could never go back to England?

"The phoneutria fera. Its meaning in Greek," he clarified, seeing something that I hoped he thought was confusion on my face.

He was just showing off that he'd done his homework. I cleared my throat. "The female often kills the male following mating if they don't make a quick enough getaway." I shrugged. "It's actually quite common in the arachnid world."

"I'm sure glad I'm not a phoneutria fera then." Guy grinned and sipped his wine.

Feeling the rinse of relief, I laughed a little too loudly and a little too long.

Guy told me he was from Pennsylvania, north of Philadelphia, some place of importance in the American Revolution that he explained but I didn't quite catch. He'd read finance at university and worked for years on Wall Street. After making "a good chunk of change," as he put it, he decided he wanted to do something different. I'd slowed my drinking as he talked about himself. I needed mental acuity to detect anything that didn't seem to mesh with what I'd read online. But it all did, perfectly. I relaxed.

He suddenly stabbed the table with a forefinger. "Rowena, I want you to understand something about me right up front. I believe that nature is the key to improving millions of lives. Instead of manufacturing ridiculously expensive drugs that are available to few, we should use what our planet produces naturally and replicate that all over the world, so medicines are available to everyone. We need to start a rebel pharmaceutical movement."

Good god, had he found that article I wrote for some obscure university publication? "I used to say exactly the same thing when I was a student, but I discovered battling big companies is a rather grandiose ambition."

"Hey, no one ever achieved anything by thinking small," he said with that grin. "I believe in the law of the jungle — you can be the predator or the prey."

"Is that also the law of the business world, then? Be predator or prey?"

"Absolutely."

By the time we broached the subject of Guy's business proposal, we'd finished the wine and Guy was on his second scotch.

"That was my father's preferred drink." I was amazed at the uncanny confluences of interest that the night was unspooling.

"I generally go for single malt neat, but I'll take what I can get here."

We were the only diners left and the waiters hovered around the perimeter of the room, not bothering to disguise their yawns.

Guy looked around uncertainly. "It's not that late, is it?"

"People get going at sunrise in the tropics. It's the coolest part of the day."

He swallowed the rest of his drink and made a scribbling motion in the air at the waiter to request the bill.

We arranged to meet the following morning back at the restaurant. "To be continued," Guy said.

Nestled in the hollow of my mattress, his words and face floated around me on a cloud of giddiness. It was just the lubrication of alcohol, I told myself. Then it occurred to me that it could even be a hallucinogenic flashback from the yopo I'd regularly consumed for a decade and a half. But when I awoke in the morning buoyant of spirit at the thought of seeing him again, I dismissed my trepidation. I liked him, this Guy Westerphal, angel investor.

"So Rowena, what do you need to finish the research as soon as possible?" Guy rested his coffee cup within its circle in the saucer after exchanging preliminaries on how we slept and so forth.

I felt a twitch of nerves, but I had to be candid. "My research permit is under re-evaluation to determine if my study meets the government's socialist mission. All foreign projects are under review. To be perfectly blunt, I don't think mine will pass muster unless I have money to pay bribes. American dollars, cash, preferably."

He waved his hand as if it were a trifle. "Done."

Well, that was surprisingly easy. "Of course, I need funding to finish my research, but I live simply in the jungle and the raw materials are essentially free. The real cost will be in human trials and getting it to market."

Guy nodded. "How long do you estimate before the formula is ready?"

"The better part of a year."

"No problem. What else?"

He was like a genie unleashed from the bottle, but here was the big test. Based on what he'd said at dinner about a "rebel pharmaceutical movement," I'd decided, during my walk to the hotel, to up my demand. I drew a deep breath.

"I want twelve percent of the profits to create a research station to help indigenous tribes defend themselves against loggers and poachers and continue scientific inquiry into the medicinal properties of jungle fauna and flora."

The most that companies had ever wanted to give was a measly two percent, although I had managed to cajole the last one into going up to a whole three percent, but only after R&D costs had been covered. I'd accepted, but then the company withdrew the deal through a loophole.

I continued my well-practiced declamation. "I need a meaningful amount to create an immediate income stream because there's simply no time to lose. The Amazon rainforest, the lungs of planet Earth visible even from space, is rapidly losing ground to the forces of so-called civilization. If we don't act now . . ."

I halted. Guy had steepled his hands and was staring into his coffee cup. I'd lost him. I gazed at the gorgeous, and rare, hyacinth macaw that was pecking at its dish of papaya chunks and banana slices nailed to a tall stand. I'd cocked it up. Again. What was I doing that was so wrong? I slumped back in my chair, unsure how to rescue the plan.

Then Guy's head jerked up, his eyes fever bright.

"That's our branding. We'll have a rainforest logo, and our advertising will feature the conservation station in the jungle. We'll use the station to develop a whole line of natural products derived from the rainforest. I bet we can get a bunch of celebrity tree-huggers and Instagram influencers on board. It's a brilliant plan, Rowena!"

Fireworks exploded in my chest. For the first time, someone had seen that my dream was purposeful, worthwhile, not some eccentric interest that had to be tolerated or discouraged.

"Right then," I said, feeling a gust of enthusiasm.

Guy sighed. "You Brits. You're so damn underwhelmed all the time, you kill me. I'll get my lawyer in Miami to start wiring the funds and write up the agreement. But before I get carried away with that, I need to buy some presents for my daughter. I promised to bring her back souvenirs."

"You have a daughter?"

"She'll be twelve in a few months. She's the reason I'm doing all this, so she can be proud of her old dad."

"And her mother?" I said before I could stop myself. "If you don't mind my asking."

Guy turned down his mouth and rolled his eyes. "Not the reason I'm doing this." He brightened and changed the subject, which I took to mean the daughter's mother was a sore one. "Why don't you come with me? I could use a woman's input."

Shopping was hardly my forté, but I felt reluctant to surrender his companionship. "I think there's a handcrafts market somewhere."

The hotel clerk gave us directions to the market where Guy bought an assortment of knick-knacks, wood carvings of jungle animals — toucan, jaguar, tapir, and anteater — a feather crown, a miniature tribal hut, and a T-shirt. I enjoyed myself immensely.

As we walked back to his hotel, laden with parcels, the open display of Guy's thoughtfulness for his daughter triggered a wave of urgent longing for my own father. I felt the nettle sting of tears as memories washed over me. Sitting on a bench swinging my legs and licking cones of Cornish ice cream as we watched cold surf crashing on the rocks, the cream teas on my birthdays, eating a hot pastie out of a paper bag after a ramble. Until he had a coronary whilst we were driving along a cliffside road and hurtled to his death. I, for some reason, emerged from the crash unscathed.

The previous night Mum and Dad had a big quarrel, the subject of which was me. Dad wanted to send me to a good boarding school, but Mum had protested. Lying in bed, I'd heard it all through the thin walls of our bungalow.

"It'll never work. She's odd, Malcolm. She doesn't get on with other children."

"You only want her to work in your garden, keep her as your slave to pull weeds. She needs to get away from you, then she won't be so odd."

"What about you?" Mum shrieked. "What about you?! What do you two get up to all alone on the moors then? You want to put her in boarding school, so you'll have an excuse to have dirty weekends together in a hotel."

"You're revolting, Adelaide, utterly sick."

The next morning, he complained of tightness in his chest, which he often had following stressful incidents. Most involved my mother. Mum made up a tisane for him. It wasn't until years later that I fully remembered and understood the events of that night and the following day.

I was finishing my studies at Oxford and telling my mother of my plan to go to South America. She threw one of her wobblies, saying that she had put me through university so I could help her expand her medicine business. "Selfish, that's what you are. Just like your father." Bitterness saturated her voice. "You weren't even supposed to live, you know that Rowena?"

Everything twigged in a momentous blast of illuminative clarity. I suddenly knew what the extra vial on the kitchen table that fateful morning was, next to my father's usual herbal heart remedy that had hawthorn and motherwort as its principal ingredients. As my mother put the kettle on and set about making an infusion to ease Dad's arrythmia, she saw me enter the kitchen and swiftly secreted the vial into her apron pocket. All I could make out was "Mo . . ." on the label. I thought nothing of it. Mum was always playing around with different herbal combinations. But at that moment years later, I knew. It was monkshood root, which boasted beautiful blue cowl-shaped flowers and was highly poisonous.

She'd murdered my father, knowing that no postmortem toxicology report would detect monkshood unless it was specifically sought, which it wouldn't be as he had arrhythmia and family history of heart problems. She'd also sought to kill me, getting two for the price of one like a sale on socks at Marks & Spencer, but it hadn't quite worked according to her plan.

Rage surged, reminding me that the knot of anger that had formed that day was still inside me. After my act to right the scales of justice, I'd expected it to vanish. And I thought it had. But in fact, I'd simply grown more skillful at submerging it deeper where it had hardened into an immutable tumor. My tears receded into my eyes. Anger was a handy way to dispatch weepiness.

"Rowena, what is it?" Guy said.

He was staring at me. My cheeks grew hot. "Seeing you doing things for your daughter made me think of my own father. Silly of me."

"Not in the least." He curled an arm around my shoulders and gave me a clumsy one-sided hug. It felt comforting. "It happens like that sometimes. The wrong person dies. Life is unfair."

I looked at him with a strengthened sense of connection. "That's what angers me the most, the bloody unfairness of everything. People make life unjust. They just bugger it up all the time."

"I can't argue with that." He clutched my shoulder again. "Come on. I'll buy you a drink. Shopping's hard work."

We entered the bar of his hotel. His tongue soon loosened by whisky, he confided that he too had suffered an abysmal childhood. His parents had been poor, his father never able to keep a job as simple as cutting lawns and his mother spinning elaborate stories that she was the illegitimate offspring of European royalty, but 'the family' had blocked her from claiming her rightful inheritance. One day, she pledged, she'd force them to admit her into their ranks and she'd whisk Guy off to live in a palace with crystal chandeliers in every room, a massive freezer filled with all the flavors of ice cream known to man and a brand-new outfit to wear every day.

"Now, of course, it sounds obviously delusional, but growing up I believed every word. When I was fifteen, she died in a psychiatric hospital, choked on her own vomit in a spit mask. I lost contact with my father as soon as I could. No idea where he is. The day I walked out of that shitbox of a house, I vowed I'd never live a small life."

Good god. I had no idea what to say so I simply squeezed his hand lying on the table. He squeezed mine back, then his face broke into a grin.

"Did I ever tell you about the time I tried to surf in Hawaii?"

He soon had me laughing at his mishaps riding the waves off Oahu. I suddenly realized how diminished my world had become. Being with Guy was like throwing open a shuttered window and letting an ocean breeze blow out the stale air.

The lawyer sent the agreement from Miami, and we signed and notarized it. After that, the first allotment of money arrived quickly. Armed with a full purse, I was able to persuade Clodo to secure an appointment for me with YOU at the Institute, as well as surreptitiously move myself to more presentable lodgings. Guy had already asked where I was staying. Embarrassed, I'd fobbed him off with a vague answer. YOU (Guy said I had quite the sense of humor) was quite appreciative of the size of the cash donation, which she immediately swept into the top drawer of her desk and assured me my permit would be ready in a fortnight. She even shook my hand.

We started purchasing supplies: chemistry equipment that I'd made do without, crates of nonperishable foodstuffs such as powdered milk and eggs, instant coffee, tea and tinned meats, bottled water, iodine tablets to purify rainwater, medicines including antimalarial tablets, and toiletries: soaps, toothpaste and shampoo, mosquito nets for sleeping and repellent, paraffin for lamps. After I told Guy I'd had to sell my boat some months ago to raise funds and was hitching lifts with my neighbors when they went to town to sell baskets and crops, he insisted on buying a new metal longboat and outboard engine. "You can't be without your own transportation, Rowena."

He spared no expense. When he saw where I was rooming, my new hotel that felt quite sumptuous, he immediately wanted to upgrade me to the five-star hotel where he was staying. (Thank God he hadn't seen the old place!) "Oh no," I said. "That's too much."

"You're blushing, Rowena. If you don't mind my saying so, you look cute when you blush."

My face boiled. I studied the scruffy toes of my boots.

"Now you're even redder and even cuter."

"I don't believe that particular adjective has ever been applied to me." I was still unable to raise my head.

"Now you'll definitely remember me then."

"You're quite memorable as it is, Guy."

He chortled. "Good. I aim to be."

I finally looked up. "I could use a pair of new boots though."

He laughed again. "Now you're talking. Let's find a shoe store. No offense, but you could use some new clothes, too."

"None taken." My khakis were worn to the point of fraying.

He didn't haggle with me or ask me to justify any purchase. "Believe me, your startup costs are nothing. I've had twenty-three-year-olds who think investors should pay for massages and well-being coaches and interior decorators."

Guy's acceptance of me, his treatment of me as an equal, was like a transfusion of oxygenated blood into my being. It was so unlike working with the R&D scientists. They'd always come in pairs, questioned everything I did, exchanged furtive glances or raised eyebrows when they thought I wasn't looking. At night, I'd hear them murmuring in their hut, undoubtedly gossiping about me, like the children all through my school years. To my neighboring tribe and in San Carlos, too, I was and would always be the outsider, the foreigner, no matter how long I lived there. Now at night, as I lay in my comfy bed, I thought that perhaps there was some sort of karmic wheel of justice. Finally, I was not only gaining recognition, I was fitting in, belonging, in a way that I never had.

Everything was finally ready. We'd accumulated numerous pallets of supplies and had them covered with loose nets and transferred onto a cargo boat heading downriver to be delivered in care of Carlota. I collected the new research permit from the Institute and arranged my passage to San Carlos for the following day.

We celebrated with a bottle of sparkling wine at the hotel restaurant where we'd become regular diners as we discussed plans for the conservation station and other possible products we could launch. The eve of my departure, however, our mood was somber.

"I've really enjoyed working with you over the past two weeks, Row." Guy had taken to abbreviating my name to a single syllable, which I'd always detested, but somehow didn't mind coming from him. It seemed a sign of affection.

"As have I with you." A stone of dread formed in the pit of my stomach. As of tomorrow, I'd be on my own again.

"We make a perfect team, wouldn't you say?" Guy said.

I nodded, grabbing the saltshaker and tapping it on the table, both to disguise the rawness of my feelings and to loosen the salt, which clumped with humidity. I'd really never liked working alongside people, until now. "Humans are social animals," I remembered Professor Medford-Jones saying one evening as he was holding court with postgraduate students at his local, The Rose & Thistle. "We prefer to be with people like ourselves. We're tribal like that." I'd always pooh-poohed that concept, but now I saw the truth of it.

"I'm going to miss you," Guy said.

A spear pierced my heart, and I concentrated on the saltshaker. My voice dropped to just above a whisper. "I think . . . I think I'll miss you too." I'd never voiced such a sentiment to anyone.

"I'm glad to hear you say that." He leaned forward. "I've been thinking, how about I come and live at the camp while you finish the research?"

I looked up at him, somewhat astounded. "It's extremely primitive living. I don't know if . . ."

"I can help you and that will move things faster. Besides, I want to get a handle on what this conservation station would look like."

I pondered for a second. I couldn't think of any reason why he shouldn't come. We were partners, after all. He probably should see and experience everything. There were a few things I didn't especially want him to see, but I could hide them.

"That would be lovely."

He raised his glass in a toast and as I held my glass to his, our gaze fused in the pearly candlelight. I felt a flutter in my chest, like the beating wings of hummingbirds. In that moment, my life changed irrevocably.

PART II

In a prop plane, we flew two hundred and sixty miles south of Puerto Ayacucho following the path of Rio Negro, a serpentine dark ribbon that formed the border between Venezuela and Colombia in this region.

Guy leaned into the window. "What makes the water black?"

"Humic acid caused by the incomplete breakdown of vegetation containing phenol. It's really more of a tea color but it looks black from a distance."

He shook his head with a bemused smile. "Row, you're a walking encyclopedia."

I smiled back. I was still astonished that this was all real.

Carlota met us at the dirt airstrip, which viewed from above looked like a claw mark in the jungle's ochre earth. She'd taken charge of the supplies that had arrived by boat and arranged an aquatic caravan to transport the cargo to camp. Four long narrow boats, including our new smaller one, awaited us already loaded.

"Is it my imagination or is it even hotter and more humid here than in Puerto Ayacucho?" Guy's face was scarlet as if I'd colored it with one of my crayons.

"We're one degree north of the Equator here. Ayacucho is six degrees north. Not much of a difference. You'll cool off once we get going in the boat," I said.

I sensed a shift in our dynamic. Now we were on my territory, which meant I was the one in charge. Hands on his hips, Guy looked around. Stray dogs, one with her swollen teats almost touching the ground, sniffed a rubbish heap. Small houses with rusty corrugated iron roofs lined the road. Locals, skin as tanned as leather, walked around in shorts, loose shirts, baseball caps and flip-flops. The beat of salsa music sounded faintly from an invisible source. Compared to even Puerto Ayacucho, it looked pretty rough, I had to admit.

"This is really the biggest town in the region?" he said.

I nodded. "It's surrounded by pure forest. Colombia's across the river to the north. Ecuador's to the southwest and a little further southeast on our side of the river, Brazil. The Rio Negro joins the Amazon in Manaus. It's quite a sight to behold actually. The rivers maintain their colors, black and brown, alongside each other for quite a way until they blend."

He pointed to a cell phone tower and huge satellite dish on top of a roof. "It's not entirely cut off then."

"There's a new internet café down the road." Carlota signaled the main street paved with interlocking cement bricks. "But you won't be able to get mobile phone or internet where you'll be." She turned to me. "By the way, your box of jam arrived. It's on the boat."

Guy gave me a quizzical look.

"I confess to being partial to marmalade and gooseberry jam. Carlota orders it from the UK for me through her Miami postal service."

"I warn you; she eats it with everything." Carlota smiled.

"I was wondering what bad habits you had," Guy said good-naturedly. "Well, off we go then."

The boatmen pushed the prows of the boats off the sand into the water and jumped in. We did the same with our boat.

"You'd think the town would have a jetty of some kind," Guy said.

I shrugged as I took control of the outboard engine handle. "One thing you learn about living in these places, you don't need even half of what you left behind. It's incredibly freeing."

I took the lead position in our caravan. Being the lightest boat, we were the speediest. We thrummed along the river, purling the water into V-shaped wedges in our wakes. As we rocketed along, I inhaled deeply, reveling in the familiar rank edge that river water gave to the air. A caiman slithered into the river with nary a splash. A tree was alive with chattering green parrots. I held up my hand to greet a boat crammed with people and bamboo cages containing hens and piglets on their way to town. An old woman stared back with an impassive face from under a black umbrella she held as a parasol.

I was awed at my reversal of fortune. I had left the jungle a month ago under armed escort by the National Guard and fraught with tension. I was returning with a broad new horizon shining with promise as never before.

"You weren't kidding when you said this place was remote," Guy shouted over the full-throated roar of the boat engine.

"Won't be long now," I shouted back.

"You said that an hour ago."

I replied with a beatific smile and thrust my face into the warm windshear. Nothing could rock the happiness that seemed as if it were radiating from my very marrow.

After nearly two hours, I throttled the engine to cut a clean arc into a narrow channel and we sliced through a flitting cloud of iridescent blue morphos butterflies. We made the second turn into an alley of water narrowed by overhangs of dense foliage and slowed to a chug. Without the windshear, the air clung to our skin like honey.

A sandy alcove emerged into view, and exultation filled me. I smiled at Guy, wanting him to share my exhilaration, but he was busy absorbing his new surroundings.

We putted in and banked the boats. Children ran out and swarmed around me in barefoot glee. "Rowena! Rowena!" I gathered them in a sweeping embrace.

A wizened old woman hobbled out from a hut. Her lower jaw moved as if she was chewing her gums, which had long lost their teeth. Her eyes bore the milky film of cataracts. I greeted her in Nheengatu. She smiled, recognizing my voice, and told me the men were off hunting and the women tilling the cassava fields behind the settlement.

"They're wearing regular clothes," Guy said. "I thought they'd be in loincloths with sticks through their noses."

"You're thinking of the Yanomamo. They're quite a bit further inland, not near any town at all."

"I wouldn't exactly call this close to town," Guy muttered.

I introduced him. "This is Guy. He's going to be helping me with my research." The youngsters stopped their clamor and, fingers hooked in their mouths, stared at the large stranger.

The boatmen had unloaded the cargo onto the shore and awaited further orders.

"Children, you'll get your presents if you help bring supplies to the camp." I motioned to the boatmen, who hoisted boxes onto their shoulders. The kids grabbed small parcels.

I felt like the Pied Piper of Hamelin as we set off down the path through the brush to my camp. The atmosphere was vaporous with the air trapped under the thick tree canopy. The only light came from sun streaming through slats in the jungle awning like the illustrations of divine presence in my father's old Bibles. Birds cooed unseen in the trees. The forest had already reclaimed the path in patches. I'd have to get at it with my machete.

"When you said your camp is next to the village, how far did you mean?" Guy said after a couple of minutes.

"It's exactly a seven-minute walk."

"I thought you said your camp was on the river. We couldn't have pulled the boats up closer?"

"That's where the boat landing is."

I hoped he wasn't going to continue whingeing. We entered the clearing of my camp. As the boatmen dropped their loads and returned for another load, I hastened to the phoneutria fera's hut. I hoped they were still alive, but a quick check of the glass tanks sitting on the rudimentary benches I'd constructed confirmed my fears. I turned to Guy, whose shadow filled the threshold.

"Bit of a setback, I'm afraid. We're going to have to harvest new spiders."

"What happened?"

"When I didn't return after a few days, the villagers probably believed that I'd left for good, so they didn't bother to feed them. They don't like the phoneutria fera and with good reason. The bites are nasty although seldom lethal. The erections men get can be quite painful and last five hours or so."

He peered into the tanks. I picked up a dead specimen so Guy could get a good look at one. Hairy and light brown in color, its eight legs stretched across my palm.

"You probably don't think they're ugly, do you?" he said.

"I don't actually. Everything in the animal kingdom has evolved with purpose. I see the harmonious symmetry of nature when I look at them."

"Will getting new ones take long?"

"It really depends. They're nocturnal so we'll have to go out at night."

He sighed with exasperation.

I walked out, feeling a twist of angst that he was upset, but it wasn't my fault. In the pile of boxes, I found the one containing the trinkets for the children, plastic whistles, cars, soldiers and animals, and I handed them out. They ran back to the village with their new treasures.

"Let's have the tour then. Where's the lab?" Guy said.

I stood. He obviously thought there was more to the camp than four huts. I walked him over to another hut. "This is the sleeping quarters."

He peered rather dubiously into the interior, which consisted of one pole in the middle. "What exactly do we sleep on?"

I pointed to the canvas hammocks hanging folded on the pole. "We hang up the hammocks at night with mosquito nets over us. Clothing and other belongings I put in those netting bags and hang them from the rafters so snakes and whatnot don't get into them. You can sleep in the storeroom. There's plenty of space."

I pulled down the metal box from its cubbyhole.

"This is where I store all my research notes and important papers to try to keep the humidity at bay. It's never entirely successful." I opened the lid and showed him the plastic bags inside. "Put your passport and any other important document in one of these sealed bags."

"Moldy papers. Great," he mumbled.

I led him outside and into another hut. "This is the storeroom." The tinned goods I'd left on the shelves were gone. The villagers had likely been on a raid. I couldn't blame them.

"What's all this?" He pointed to a shelf containing palm-leaf pouches. He put one to his nose, took a whiff and scrunched his face in distaste.

I smiled. "That's my medicine cabinet I told you about. The old woman you met taught me all about plant remedies. They work for a surprisingly wide variety of ailments."

He put back the pouch. "I'm glad we bought first aid supplies. Bathroom?"

"There's an outhouse of sorts, a hole in the ground down a little trail, but don't worry, it's screened in. For bathing and washing and so on, I collect rainwater in a big tank. The bathing area is another little private cubicle."

"Okaaay. Dare I ask where the lab is?"

I pointed to an open-sided pavilion with a wooden plank floor and a roof supported by poles. A long bench divided the space down the middle.

"The kitchen's at the far end." I pointed to some shelving containing a few blackened pots, a wooden table and a couple of the ubiquitous cheap, molded plastic armchairs. A plastic tub on a tree stump served as the sink. Something was missing.

"Bugger. Looks like someone's gone off with my propane cooker." I checked around, but it was gone. I sighed. "Well, I suppose it was too good to be true, that nothing would've been nicked in my absence."

"Who would've taken it?"

"The villagers, boatmen, even the guardsmen could've returned."

Guy scratched his neck. "Row, this is beyond primitive. This is Stone Age."

The cold spear of fear pricked me. "Are you having second thoughts? I did try to warn you."

"I'll get used to it. Let's get everything unpacked." The resignation in his voice chipped my happiness. I didn't want him to feel resigned. I wanted him to want to be here.

As we sorted out the camp, Guy fell unusually silent. He seemed distant, answering only with morose monosyllables. He was regretting coming, thinking about leaving, I thought. I blamed myself. I should've told him more forcefully not to come. I should've been more upfront about living conditions at the camp. I hadn't realized that he wouldn't know what jungle living really meant. I was so used to it that I hadn't really considered it from his vantage point. I'd been selfish in agreeing so readily because I wanted his company.

When night fell, he grabbed a granola bar and retired to his hammock and mosquito net in the storeroom that I'd helped him rig up, saying he was exhausted. I took an oats granola bar and dipped it in the pot of marmalade to eat it and climbed into my own hammock. I wasn't looking forward to the next day. Guy surely would make his departure and I'd be on my own again. The prospect saddened me. I realized that in the space of just a few weeks, I'd become clingy, allowed myself to grow reliant on Guy. Perhaps I'd needed company more than I thought.

I needed to collect myself. I got out of the hammock and took out one of the special adult coloring books and boxes of crayons, which Carlota ordered for me on the internet, and a flat board that served as a desk. By the dim light of a paraffin lamp, I hung from a pole, I sat in the hammock and colored mandalas with vivid shades until I felt my eyelids grow leaden.

At sunrise the next day, I got up, feeling heavy with the weight of expected bad news, gathered some stones into a circle and laid a fire in the middle with an old grill resting on the stones over it. I was just setting the kettle on it to boil bottled water for tea for me, instant coffee for Guy, when I heard Guy's voice behind me.

"Good morning."

I returned the greeting with a wan smile.

"Row, I've been thinking."

"I know. You're leaving. It's too primitive."

He screwed up his face. "No, nothing like that. But we're going to make some changes." A burden lifted from my shoulders like a magic spell. He took a notepad out of the breast pocket of his shirt and flipped it open.

"Why don't we pay the villagers to get us a new batch of phoneutria fera? I'll give a good amount for each spider."

"God, they'll be thrilled."

"Good. I also took a look at the riverbank just now. I'll pay them to clear the brush away so we can have our own boat landing. It doesn't make sense to be lugging stuff through the jungle."

"Right."

"I also noticed an old generator down by the outhouse."

I winced. "I had to stop using it due to the cost of fuel. It's probably unusable by now."

"I'll take a look at it now and see if it'll still run. If not, I'm going into town today and ordering us a new one and plenty of fuel, as well as a fan. I'll also get a new portable stove with two burners and propane, and whatever else we need."

"Guy, that would be . . ."

"No need to thank me, Row. I'm here to look after you. There's nothing for you to worry about ever again."

His words moved me. That, combined with relief that he was staying, caused me to tear up.

"What's the matter?"

"I was afraid you were planning to leave."

He grabbed me by the upper arms. This time I collapsed against his chest, shuttered my eyes and inhaled the tang of his sweat. I felt his arms snake around me, his hands palpating the small of my back.

"You don't mind, do you?" he whispered close to my ear, his breath warm.

My heart galloped. I shook my head, afraid that if I spoke, I'd ruin the moment.

"You can put your arms around me," he murmured. "I'd like that."

Timidly, I slid my hands around his waist. When my arms had encircled him, he tightened his embrace and then I felt his hand on my chin tilting my face slowly upward. Keeping my eyes firmly shut, I allowed him to lead me, still afraid that my full participation in what I hoped was about to come would spoil the present and jinx the future.

Then I felt it, the soft pressure of his lips on mine. The world dropped away in that moment and the only thing that existed was our mutual touch. It lasted a second or two, then he drew away, brushing his forefinger along my cheek.

"I better take a look at that generator, or we won't get anything accomplished today."

I smiled. "I'll prepare for the trip."

"Oh, you stay here and organize the spider hunt and the brush clearing. I'll head into town. Just give me directions."

"Right then. I'll have coffee ready in a jiffy."

He set off down the path and I busied myself with the Nescafé.

Three-quarters of an hour later, I was helping him shove off our boat into the channel. He clambered in, started the engine and blew me a kiss as he turned the boat. I waved and blew him a kiss back. He had directions, which consisted of three turns in waterways, and a shopping list, including the generator, shoved in his pocket. I trudged up to the village and set about getting the tasks going. A group of men showed up at the camp a little while later with their machetes. I carted off the brush as they slashed and uprooted.

By midday, we had cleared a small space on the shore amid the bushes, enough for the boat. Guy will be pleased, I thought. In the late afternoon as I waited for him to arrive, I inserted my favorite disc of Strauss waltzes on my battery-powered CD player and worked on more humidity-warped pages in the coloring book. It was a remarkably soothing, all-encompassing activity. When I was engaged in coloring with orchestral melody filling my ears, I thought of nothing else. I inhaled the waxy smell as I applied pinks, purples, yellows, reds, blues to bring outlined illustrations of intricate designs to life. I never used greens or browns since those hues made up my world. I gave those crayons to the village children, who were delighted with them.

My penchant for coloring started two years previously when I finally gave up my longtime yopo habit. I'd tried several times over the course of fifteen years to give up the hallucinogenic seeds, which I ground into a powder and inhaled via a foot-long bamboo tube, as a Piaroa shaman deep in the Alto Orinoco had taught me. The result was an hours-long, trance-like dissociative state that freed my mind and provided unparalleled access to the subconscious. In the midst of panoramic kaleidoscopic scenes, I passed hours floating with my dear father, communicating with our hearts not words. I would be enraptured by music played by enormous sunflowers, swaddled in pillowy loaves of perfume, dancing balletic whirligigs with tireless feet upon oceans of nourishing, cherishing love.

Yopo was my salvation, giving me everything reality had not and of course could not. With little other distraction in my hermitic life, it seduced and obsessed me like a lover. I went through repeated cycles of heavy use and abstinence, as much to reverse the effects of tolerance as anything since I was consuming quite a bit of the stuff, but the lure of psychedelic nirvana always reeled me back in. This went on for years until the anodyne trances abruptly turned into what I could only describe as psychotic, demonic nightmares literally of Dantesque proportions. In the first journey, I was trapped in the Seventh Circle of Hell where murderers are punished by being lowered into boiling blood. It bears noting that the yopo user cannot end the cataleptic state at will. One simply has to endure it until the effect wears off.

After that horrific fugue, I gave yopo a rest until time had dulled my memory of its terrors then dosed myself again. This time, the dust became my Geryon transporting me to the Eighth Circle of Hell reserved for treachery. After ten unrelenting hours of living in a Hieronymous Bosch painting, I swore off the stuff for good. Perhaps it had short-circuited my brain in some way.

Not long after that, I idly picked up a coloring book and crayons I'd bought for the village children and began to color one evening. I discovered that when I combined the activity with music, I could lose my reality but not my brain. Thanks to Carlota, I found out that coloring books for adults and better-quality crayons existed, so she'd order me a dozen sets at a time. I hadn't told Guy about yopo. I suspected he'd seize on it as another "supplement." Nor had I told him about my puerile pastime of coloring. Everything has its moment, as my father would say.

I'd advised Guy to return before dusk. It was easy to get lost on the waterways at night, plus you didn't know what wild creatures, animal or human, you'd run into. The thought that for once, I had someone to wait for filled me to the brim.

He putted in just before the sun faded. I waded out, climbed in the boat and directed him to our new landing. He kissed the crown of my head, chuffed at the quick progress. He'd brought everything on the list. We ferried it all to camp and set it up. Soon the generator was thrumming, and a fan circulated the soupy air. Guy sat in front of the warm breeze, his head craned back with his eyes closed.

"Not exactly AC, but it's better than nothing." He held up a plastic tumbler of scotch, which I'd advised him to stock up on in Puerto Ayacucho before we left.

"The women are going out to hunt for the spiders tonight," I said. "The men don't want to go in case they get bitten, given the venom's effects on males."

"Excellent." Guy hoisted his cup. "Here's to teamwork."

"Hear, hear." I toasted with a tepid beer that he'd brought from town.

After I cleared away our dinner of omelettes made from powdered eggs, he maneuvered my chair next to his and spread his arm across the back like a wing. I sat down and he drew me to him, cupping my face in his hands. This time, our lips parted. I felt a trill of nerves. I knew the next step would come sooner rather than later. I was ready. It had always struck me as an irony of ironies: I was researching an instinctual human interaction with which I'd had pitifully little practical experience. I wasn't a virgin. Clifford Peever had seen to that. But then, I had seen to Clifford Peever.

My one and only romance, if one could call it that, had occurred during my first year at Oxford. Cliff, a classmate in a course on French existentialist literature, initiated it during a Friday night at the pub. Cliff had cornered me as I was coming out of the toilets, pushed me up against the wall, pawed my breasts and rammed his tongue down my throat. I was taken aback but also flattered. The only interest boys had ever taken in me was to call me names, weirdo, freak and the like. So, when Cliff invited me to his bedsit at closing, I accepted. And there it happened on his unwashed sheets. A painful thrust and it was over. At least it was quick, I thought, but hardly worth the raves that I'd heard from other girls. Still, after I left Cliff snoring and walked home in the dark, I rejoiced in the fact that I now had a boyfriend, that I was like those other girls.

I soon noticed, though, that Cliff didn't ask me to go places with him. In fact, he barely spoke to me. Our interludes only came in the lubricated atmosphere of the pub, where they followed a predictable pattern. He'd find me by the loo. We'd return separately to our table, full of our secret dalliance, then I'd go back to his flat at closing, leaving separately from the pub and meeting down at the corner to walk the rest of the way. There'd be a quick coupling, he'd fall asleep, and I'd go home. I thought he was simply shy. I asked him once if he'd like to go to the cinema, but he mumbled something and slinked off. I had to give him a chance, I thought. He'd warm up.

After a month or so of this routine, a girl in my literature class took me aside one day and informed me that Cliff's bedding of me was the result of a bet he'd made with friends to see who could go home with the "plainest girl," which was how she euphemistically put it.

"He's using you, Rowena." She showed me a forwarded text conversation on her mobile.

> Unknown sender: You still shagging that cow?
> Cliff: Ugly girls are the best, bro. They're so easy because they're desperate! I'm going to have to end it though. She actually asked me to hang out with her the other day. Not fuckin likely!

I was gobsmacked.

"I'm so sorry, Rowena. It's just awful, but I thought you should know."

"Thanks ever so . . ." I managed to spit out then I turned and ran. When I was alone by the bins in an alley, I burst into tears. All the insults I'd endured assaulted me. My mother telling me I was no good, ugly, a ninny that no one would ever want. Children at school. Even teachers. "She's a peculiar little thing, isn't she? Very bright, of course, but so . . .

socially clumsy." I'd thought I'd left all that behind me, would have a fresh start at Oxford. But it was happening again. I felt pillaged.

Why did people have to pick on me, or on anyone for that matter? Why couldn't they let others be? It wasn't fair. I'd always let it go, as Dad said. That was his strategy with Mum. When she launched into one of her tirades, shouting that she'd married a mouse not a man, he'd clear his throat, look at his shoes and rock on his heels with his hands clasped behind his back. It wound her up even more, pushed her to goad him into reacting. His other tactic was avoiding her as much as possible, although with a similar effect when he finally did come home. I'd done the same when dealing with bullies. I'd remain in the school library studying whilst other children gamboled in the playground.

But this time, I thought as I jerked my cardigan sleeve across my moist cheeks, this time I was going to handle it differently. I'd be like Mum. I would not turn the other cheek.

It was Thursday. I had to move fast since I met Cliff on Fridays. I skived off my classes the next day and caught an early train home. I waited until my mother closed the shop and went home for lunch. I let myself in the back door with the spare key hidden under a pot of geraniums, found what I was looking for and jogged back to the station just in time for the return express.

The evening unfolded as usual, but I stuck to drinking shandies to keep my wits about me, then I ordered a pint of foamy bitter, Cliff's drink, waited until he'd almost finished the one in his hand, then went around to where he was sitting and slid the fresh glass in front of him.

"My treat, Cliff."

His friends sniggered, and he looked bashful. I smiled grandly. I went back to my seat and kept an eye on him. When he'd almost finished the beer, I got up and waited for him by the toilets. He went to slobber over me as usual, but I cut him short. "Let's dispense with the preliminaries and go to your place."

When we got to his flat, he started undressing then promptly vomited. Expecting that at any moment, I'd stayed at a safe distance. Sitting in a kitchen chair, I watched with satisfaction as he dropped to the floor retching and convulsing. Soon he was curled up like a pasty white cat, the contents of his stomach lying in spatters around him. I tied a handkerchief around my nose for the smell.

I'd given him a largeish dose of acetum lobeliae, vinegar made of lobelia, also known by the descriptive monikers of pukeweed, gagroot and vomitwort. He was going to be quite ill for the weekend, but he'd recover.

"What the fucking hell did you give me?" he muttered, slimed with cold sweat as he pulled himself up onto his bed.

"Whatever do you mean? You must've caught a nasty bug. I must be off. I don't want to come down with anything."

I walked tall out of his building, whipped off my hanky and binned it. I had righted the wrong done me, balanced the scales, turned unfairness into fairness. For the first time in my life, I had seized power. And it felt fantastic. I realized that was how my mother must've felt when people who crossed her later mysteriously sickened. She'd bake biscuits, buns, cakes and other goodies and bring them in person or leave them on the doorstep as a "peace offering." I'd accompanied her on quite a few such deliveries during my childhood. It seemed such a kind, humble gesture so I was baffled when one time, the affected party approached me in the local library and told me in a fierce tone, "You tell your mother to stay the hell away from me or I'll report her." One time, a police constable actually did knock at the door. "I promise I'll be more careful to look at those sell-by dates," my mother said and then he left. It was only when I reached my teens that I twigged what she was doing. It was effective, I must say.

After Cliff, I didn't bother with men, not that there was a queue at my door, but there were a few invitations over the years, drinks, a meal, a coffee here and there. I made it clear I wasn't interested in any relationship, casual or otherwise. I couldn't see the attraction of sex anyway until Guy, who bulldozed his way into my life, first chipping away at the edges of the mound of protection I'd built on top of myself, then excavating it, exposing the raw loneliness and need that lay underneath.

Of course, my sleeping quarters weren't exactly set up for copulative activity, so our first encounter in my hammock was rather awkward. Nevertheless, thanks to Guy's purposeful effort, I finally experienced why people sought out sex with such fervor. The physical sensation was unlike any other, both during the act and afterwards as we lay like sardines in the hammock bathed in shared perspiration.

In the middle of the night, we were awakened by several women from the village. They'd been out foraging and caught a batch of six female phoneutria fera. Guy paid them in cash. Their eyes saucered when they saw the pile of banknotes in their palms, so when Guy told them in rudimentary Spanish that we needed more specimens, they nodded with zest.

At breakfast the next morning, Guy turned to me. "We need a special place for us," he said as I placed a mug of coffee on the table for him along with a plastic jar of sugar. "I'm going to talk to the village men about it."

"What do you mean?"

"You'll see." He gave a cryptic smile and spooned a generous amount of sugar into his coffee.

Within four days we had two dozen male and female specimens in the tanks and a "sex shack," as Guy had christened it. It was an open-walled lean-to with a wooden plank floor and palm-frond roof. We hung mosquito nets from the roof eaves and set on the floor two single mattresses that Guy had gone into town to purchase. He ran the fan from an extension cord attached to the generator, so we enjoyed a bit of breeze for our bedroom calisthenics. It was the jungle version of a velvet-curtained four-poster bed and deliciously decadent.

We soon settled into a routine. We rose at daybreak and after breakfast, when it was still cool, I'd head into the forest to gather beetles and other insects to feed the spiders, as I could never fully rely on what the village children caught, and also collected roots, leaves and tree barks for my cabinet of natural medicines. I explained each of them to Guy. Coagulants, analgesics, anxiolytics, anti-carcinogens, diuretics.

"We'll need cuttings or seeds of all these plants," he said in amazement. "We can develop the ones that have the most commercial medicinal potential."

I set to work milking the spider venom and once I had a good amount, isolated the Tx2-6, the priapic element. Guy hovered at my elbow, peppering me with questions about the phoneutria fera's habitat, diet and reproductive cycle, and scientific procedure, and taking copious notes. I found it irritating and exhausting to be constantly narrating what I was doing.

"I feel like I'm under surveillance, and my throat's sore with speaking so much," I complained.

"Row, we have to figure out how we're going to make this to scale. We can't go to market with a handful of spiders. We'll need a warehouse full of them. That's why I need to know all this."

I sighed. He was right, of course. "Well, we're going to need space for them to wander. Unlike other arachnids that lure prey into their webs, they walk about on the jungle floor and stun prey with their venom."

"I'm thinking we could build kind of a greenhouse inside a warehouse, replicate the rainforest habitat by controlling temperature and humidity, add the insects they eat. What do you think?"

"That would be ideal." I felt gratified by his thoughtfulness.

In the early afternoon, when the heat reached its zenith, we ate lunch and rested in the shade, then I resumed work whilst Guy labored on the seemingly endless business plan or went to the village to negotiate for various items, including cassava flour which I used to make flatbread. Before Guy, I'd grown my own cassava, a tuber root, and ground it. Guy, however, said it was a waste of my time and talent. He bought it from the village. He'd gotten quite friendly with the tribe. The men even invited him on a hunting trip one day. He was hesitant about going, but I urged him to accept. "It would be rude to turn it down. They don't take to outsiders easily."

He came back exhausted. "We caught a howler monkey, a wild boar and a weird-looking, brown hairy animal. They offered me a share of the meat, but I declined."

"Probably a capybara, the world's largest rodent but don't let that put you off. Its meat is a real delicacy. You should've taken it. Next time."

He waved his hand. "That was a one-time deal only."

We made use of our shack most days, often at my behest, much to Guy's amusement. "I'm benefitting from your pent-up demand, Row."

Guy went into San Carlos for fresh supplies two or three times a week and to use the internet to write to his daughter and take care of business affairs. She emailed him drawings and photos, which he'd print out to show me. He'd tell sweet stories about her as we sat together in the evenings.

"The first time she saw a cow, she said, 'Are those cows or bears, Daddy?' When I had my varicose veins done, she told a neighbor, 'Daddy's having his brains pulled.'" He chuckled. "I'd do anything for her. She's the best thing that ever happened to me. She made me realize there's more to life than money."

Guy actually had never showed interest in anything but money, as far as I could tell, but after all, we were in a business venture together. Still, I could relate. I was intensely focused on my work, perhaps too much. I was just discovering there was another side to myself, the feminine woman that I had long neglected.

As I listened to Guy talk about his little girl, I imagined it was my own father showing off photos and telling anecdotes. Often, I felt startled when I came back to reality with a bump.

"Your father would've been proud of you, Row," Guy said to me one evening as if reading my thoughts. "Any parent would be proud to have you as their daughter."

"My mother certainly wasn't. She was a harridan who hated me for existing, but since I did exist, I could serve her utilitarian purposes."

"Pox on her!" Guy said.

I had to laugh. Little did he know how close to the truth he was.

There were also times when I'd bridle at Guy's smothering presence and burrow into myself. He seemed to sense that and the next day he'd take off for town. For the first few hours, I appreciated my solitude. I'd take out a coloring book and put on music, but I didn't find it as fulfilling as I had before, and I'd soon tuck the book and crayons back into their hiding place under a pile of clothing in the sleeping hut. By the time the afternoon rolled around, I'd have sunk into a sour mood and ate gooseberry jam by the teaspoonful. The camp seemed dull without Guy, and the day stretched long and lusterless. What did he do all day in town? I wondered. When I heard the boat engine at dusk, I'd run down to the riverbank to greet him as if he'd been gone for a month.

One day, after a session in the shack, I rested my head on his chest and threaded my fingers through his mat of chest hair.

"How did I become so reliant so quickly on another person, me, who'd been so adamant about independence and solitude?" I mused aloud.

"You never knew what you were missing because you'd never allowed yourself these feelings before."

I stopped my fingers. He was right.

"I'm in love with you," he continued, "and if I'm not mistaken, you're in love with me." I drew back and looked up at him. "I love you, Rowena," he said with solemnity.

I felt a tremor of anxiety. The last time my father and I had gone for a ramble, we'd hiked to the top of a hill and sat on some ancient stones, taking in the misty valley beneath us. Dad had hugged me to him and told me I was the most precious thing in his life. I'd thrown my arms around his waist and clung to him. Two days later, he was dead. I couldn't help but feel a sense of apprehension at Guy's declaration.

"I feel you're . . . you're part of me, Guy."

"We're as one, Rowena, meant to be together."

In that moment, I truly felt that we were.

We were getting ready to perform trials of the Tx2-6 on monkeys. Guy had the tribe make cages out of bamboo and then capture red howlers, two males and two females. I gave the males a microdose of the Tx2-6. Within an hour, both males were furiously copulating with the surprised females.

We waited a day then gave the females the same dose. Nothing happened, so I upped the dosage and then the females were positioning themselves in front of the males.

"Holy shit!" Guy whooped. "This is fucking amazing, literally fucking amazing! We're going to bring about a new sex revolution! I'll go into town tomorrow and start the process for import-export licenses for the spiders. I'm sure it'll take another 'cash donation' on the Venezuelan side. Shit, I've got to tell Ellie."

The name jolted me. "Who's Ellie?"

A sheepish look dropped over his face then vanished as suddenly as it had appeared. "Oh, my assistant. She's handling things back in Miami."

He'd never mentioned her, but it seemed plausible that he'd employ such a person.

"You know, I wouldn't mind going with you to town," I said as Guy opened a bottle of beer and poured it into a cup for me and served a whisky for himself. We always had a plentiful supply of beer on hand. Guy often took some to the tribesmen as a way of currying favor.

"You're better off staying here. You can get more done while I'm not around bugging you."

He'd said the same thing when I said once before that I wanted to go into town. This time, I felt emboldened with our success to push the issue, just a wee bit. "What do you actually do all day there?"

He stiffened slightly, and I knew I'd said the wrong thing. "I talk to my daughter, tend to business. What do you think I do?"

"I was just wondering. I haven't been to San Carlos in ages. I used to go once a month."

He breathed heavily and looked into the distance as he sipped his drink. Then he turned to me with a plastered-on smile. "You deserve a break. Tomorrow, you'll come with me."

"Thank you."

My spirit soared, but later on I felt niggled by the exchange. I had to ask his permission to go to town? And why on earth did I thank him? Then, I felt a jolt of memory. Cliff Peever hadn't wanted to take me anywhere either. But Guy was nothing like Cliff, I reassured myself. Guy was taking care of me, and I wasn't used to being taken care of. I dismissed my unease.

Guy had become quite masterful at navigating the waterways. Wind blasting his hair straight back, he sped along, leaving passing boats rocking wildly in the cradle of his wake and causing dirty looks from boatmen. I felt ashamed, but Guy never looked over his shoulder. When we arrived in town, a boy ran over. "Señor Guy!"

"Miguelito, look after the boat for me." He ruffled the child's hair.

To my surprise, his Spanish had improved quite a bit. Guy headed to the internet café and I to the market. I purchased tomatoes, cucumbers and other fresh vegetables and, since there was no sign of Guy, I popped in to see Carlota.

She embraced me and ordered a sullen-faced maid to bring coffee. "This is a nice surprise. I was getting worried. I've seen Guy at the internet café and at the Paraíso lunching with the comandante and asked after you several times. How's everything going?"

I blushed. "Very well. We've started primate trials and the results look promising."

Her gaze lingered on me for a moment. "Wait, do I detect romance in the air?"

I nodded. What had given it away?

"I'd wondered."

The girl delivered the coffee on a silver tray. After she left, Carlota picked up her small cup, leaned back in her chair and frowned.

"Did Guy ever give you my letter?"

"What letter?" The hand raising the cup to my mouth halted mid-air.

"An email arrived for you from England, from your parents' lawyer. I printed it out, put it in an envelope and gave it to Guy to give to you. It must be well over a month ago."

A feeling of disconcertedness dropped over me like a hot towel. I put down the cup. "Oh that. I forgot all about it."

"You forgot about an inheritance from your uncle? It wasn't a lot of money, but there was a thirty-day deadline for responding, or they'd give the money to charity. When I didn't hear from you, I answered and told them to deposit the money in your account."

"I've just had so much going on." I stared at her indigenous pottery collection over her shoulder to avoid her very direct gaze. I felt guilty about lying that Guy had given me the letter and now was pinned by my prevarication. "I'm sorry and thank you."

She leaned forward and placed her cup on the table. "The thing is, I asked Guy if you had a response. He said you had enough money and to donate the inheritance. He'd obviously read the letter." I was completely at a loss for what to say. Why hadn't Guy told me this? "Rowena, if you want my advice, don't say anything about receiving the inheritance to him."

"Guy and I have no secrets." Although as I said those words, it occurred to me that Guy did have secrets. Then again, so did I. "But you're right, I'll keep it to myself for the time-being." I ventured a tremulous smile. "Is that a new pot I see in your collection?"

After asking her to order me black currant and red currant jellies, I left soon afterward to find Guy and ask him about the letter. I checked the internet café, but he wasn't there. I then proceeded to the Paraíso, the only restaurant with tablecloths in town. I positioned myself behind a large fern and checked the courtyard dining area. I spotted him with the comandante, just as Carlota had said, their plates looking like they were just finishing their meal. Steak, by the look of it. How very nice. I dithered for a moment, wondering whether to make my presence known, then I asked myself, what would Guy do? I marched in.

Guy was taken aback at my appearance but recovered well. "Rowena, I was just coming to find you. You know Comandante Arbillaga?"

We nodded at each other politely as I sat down without invitation. They made small talk for a few minutes, then the comandante stood and said he had to get back to work, thanked Guy for the lunch and took his leave.

"You never mentioned you were chumming up with the comandante." I tried to make my tone light, but it rang hollow.

"I didn't want to bother you with this trivial stuff. Never hurts to have friends in high places, part of doing business." He smiled and rubbed my forearm resting on the table.

"Does 'trivial stuff' include the letter Carlota gave you to give to me?"

He hesitated just a fraction of a second. I'd caught him off guard and felt a tiny swell of victory. He clapped his hand to his forehead.

"I completely forgot about that. It must be in my papers back at camp. I'm so sorry, Rowena. With all the excitement of the trials and everything, it slipped my mind." He grabbed my hand and pressed my palm to his lips. "Please forgive me."

It was entirely feasible that he could've forgotten. A lot had been going on, and he was completely focused on our budding business.

"Well, make sure you give me any correspondence in the future."

"Of course. It was all my fault. How about something to eat, something special?"

I ordered half a roast chicken with fried potatoes and quesillo, the Venezuelan version of flan, for dessert. For the rest of the meal, he was attentive and focused on me. It felt like we were back in Puerto Ayacucho, which seemed ages ago.

When we arrived back at camp at twilight, I asked Guy for the letter. He searched and said he couldn't find it. "I remember now." He raked his hair with his fingers. "A bag fell into the water when I was getting in the boat in town. I had a bunch of drawings from my daughter that I'd printed out at the internet café. They were ruined so I threw them away. Your letter was probably in the soggy mess."

Intuition told me that he would've mentioned losing his daughter's drawings. He loved showing them off to me. But why wouldn't he want me to have my uncle's inheritance? It would mean more money after all. Lying about it didn't make sense. He'd simply forgotten to tell me. That was all.

I tested different dosages of the Tx2-6 on the monkeys for a month, keeping them under close observation for side effects.

Guy grew impatient. "There's been nothing. How long do you have to keep sitting in front of monkey cages all day?"

"There've been no observable side effects. That doesn't mean there aren't any internal effects. We'll need to perform necropsies."

"Row, this isn't a drug. It's just a supplement. We'll have warnings on the labels to cover ourselves."

"People still ingest them. Besides, we need to carry out human trials first. Had you not thought of that?"

He stamped off and I turned back to the monkeys. I liked observing them. They were often human-like in their expressions of emotion and socialization but without all the noisome complications of human behavior. Sometime later, Guy returned smiling.

"I've got the solution. Let's get the tribe to take it. We'll pay them."

"That's massively unethical. We'd lose our research permit if we got found out, possibly thrown into prison. The Amazonian indigenous peoples have had dreadful experiences with outsiders taking their blood, DNA, even their feces to study. We're going to have to recruit subjects in San Carlos or Puerto Ayacucho, maybe Caracas."

"We'd cut our research time by weeks, months maybe, not to mention our expenses," Guy insisted.

"It's not on, Guy." I felt a tweak of pride for standing up to him.

His brows knitted in anger. I turned back to the monkeys and heard him thump away. A minute later, he was back. "What about this? We'll be the first guinea pigs. If it works on us, then we can give it to the tribe. What do you say?"

"You really don't give up, do you?"

"I usually get what I want. Is that a bad thing?"

I opened my mouth to argue against his idea, but he cut me off.

"Row, we're so close I can taste this thing. This is a major breakthrough and it's all yours." It was suddenly "all mine." What happened to "ours"? "Think of all the years and money and personal sacrifice you've put into this research. It's time to get it out into the world or we'll miss the opportunity. You have no idea what it's like out there. You've been out of civilization for years. We need to move fast. You believe in your work, don't you? Don't sabotage yourself."

I bristled. "I'm not sabotaging myself. I know this will work."

"Well, then?"

His suggestion did have merit, I had to admit. "It certainly wouldn't be the first time that a scientist experiments on herself," I said slowly.

"That's my girl." He extended his hand to me. I hesitated then took it and he pulled me upright. "Enough with the monkeys. No time like the present."

As I fetched the Tx2-6 from the storage hut, I felt the glimmer of a thrill. "Actually, I'm rather excited about trying this."

"That's the spirit."

"I'll start small, just double the dose I gave to the monkeys, but we may need quite a bit more considering the difference in body size." I prepared the dropper and the Tx2-6.

"Good. We need to find the smallest amount with the maximum effect for cost effectiveness." He snapped his fingers. "We could have a premium product with a higher dose and charge double the price."

I administered sublingual doses of a microgram to Guy and to myself. It tasted bitter. Guy screwed up his face in disgust. "We're definitely going to have to add flavoring or sugar or something."

I recorded the time and amount of our doses in a ledger, along with our temperatures, pulse, blood pressure and the time of the last meal. "Now we have to go about our business normally but pay attention to everything we feel."

Over the next week, we took Tx2-6 at the same time, gradually increasing the dosage until we started mauling each other.

"I think . . . we've nailed it." Guy panted as he lay beside me on the bench in the lab, slathered in sweat. We hadn't even made it to the shack.

"I've got the name for it. What about Neutria? From phoneutria."

"It sounds like 'nutrition,' as in good for you. It's brilliant. Neutria it is." He squeezed me around the waist. I was elated that he'd approved of my idea.

Secondary symptoms appeared limited to a half-degree increase in body temperature pre-coitus in women — "That's a great side effect! They'll be ripping their clothes off!" Guy crowed — post-coital headache in men — "Who cares what happens afterwards?" — and more frequent urination and decreased appetite in both — "A diuretic and a diet pill! This is a wonder drug!" Naked, Guy ran a victory lap around the compound with his fists high in the air like a footballer who's scored the winning goal.

"It's just us, though," I warned. "We really need a larger sample to be sure."

"Time to tap the tribe."

"It's still not a large enough sample. Ideally, we need hundreds of subjects. There are sixty-seven adults in the village, and of course they have radically different diets, immunity and so on from our intended targets."

"Everybody has the same sexual urges. I don't care who you are." He saw the disapproval on my face. "Don't worry. No one's going to find out. Look, we'll make it purely voluntary. Only those who want to do it. Let's just offer it and see what happens. Didn't you tell me that the indigenous culture has far fewer taboos on sex than we do?"

"Yes, but they also know the painful priapism that results from a bite of the Brazilian wandering spider. That could bias them against giving a neutral opinion."

"I know what'll do the trick. Leave it to me."

The next day Guy set off for town. He returned with a boatload of hammers, saws, axes, hoes, shovels, mosquito nets and repellent, antibiotics, antiparasitics, and water purification tablets. Things that the villagers coveted but couldn't often afford.

I cast a skeptical eye over the loot. "Bribes."

"Incentives," Guy said. "Back home, people get paid to participate in drug trials. Same thing. If you want to stay out of it, I'll go to the village myself."

I didn't want that. I knew how bombastic he could be and with his mishmash of Spanish and their language, who knew what he'd end up telling them. "I'll go on the condition that we give all the 'incentives' to the village as an unconditional thank you for all their help, and if anyone wants to take Neutria, they can."

"Done. Let's go tomorrow night," Guy said.

The next evening, we went to the village lugging boxes of "incentives." I explained to the villagers that I had finished my research and I'd like to share it with them. I also said we'd already tried Neutria ourselves with great success. There were lots of giggles at that. They all knew the purpose of my research. I made it clear that we were giving them the tools and medicine for all their help over the years.

Guy nudged me. "Make sure you tell them we're offering them the chance to try Neutria as a special present too."

I pursed my lips at him, but I had to admit it was a canny twist of words that might actually work. I dutifully delivered Guy's message.

Everyone flocked to the boxes. Within minutes, the presents were gone. Then an older couple pulled me aside and the husband said he and his wife would like to try Neutria. I gave them the dose and asked them to remember everything they felt. I'd return to the village in the morning to see how it went.

Guy was glum as we trudged back to camp. "Only one couple. That was disappointing."

"Just wait," I said.

When I returned to the village the next morning, I was met by a rush of people. Everyone wanted to try Neutria.

We ended up with full participation from the adults in the tribe. Over the next fortnight, I collected data from all the subjects, sometimes spending the night in their huts so I could record exactly how the drug affected them. We soon ran out of Tx2-6.

"We've only had one adverse reaction," I reported to Guy at the end of the two-week trial as he swung gently in a hammock that he'd put up between two poles in the lab. "Stomach upset in a pregnant woman."

"We'll put a warning on the label that pregnant women shouldn't take it. I think we're almost ready to take this to market."

"Ideally, we should observe for a while longer to see if adverse effects crop up with repeated use," I said.

"They've been practically inhaling the stuff for two weeks. It's fine." Guy fell silent for a moment. I knew him well enough by now to know that he was dreaming up one of his schemes. I waited. Then he spoke with urgency. "You're right. We should keep going with the trial. Tell the tribe you've run out of venom, and you need more spiders. Concentrate on making all the Tx2-6 that you can. Then you should observe them like you did with the monkeys, make sure there are no effects they haven't reported."

I was relieved that I'd bought some time and the next day told the tribe I needed more spiders. They were happy to oblige. Within days, I had more than fifty new spiders at my disposal and ten days later, working with just breaks for sleep, I had more than a full liter of Tx2-6 and was set to resume the trial.

I visited the village that evening with enough doses for the adults and at Guy's urging, I was to spend the night there to record the effects. The following day, Guy was going into town to purchase more gifts. I'd see him when he returned at dusk.

In the morning, I returned to camp, set purified water on to boil for tea and tidied my notes. I was a little haggard from the late night, but serene and content. My dream was coming true. After all these years, it was unbelievable, and all thanks to a chance encounter in Puerto Ayacucho when I was at my lowest point. When I saw the comandante next, I'd be sure to thank him for forcibly removing me from my camp. I soon flopped into the lab hammock and dozed off.

I awoke with a roiling in the pit of my stomach. The baked light of afternoon coated the camp. The jungle was strangely silent. No birds cooing or wild pigs rustling. I slipped out of the hammock. No Guy. Where was he? I followed the path to the riverbank and startled a thirsty capybara who scurried into the thicket. The boat landing was empty. Guy must've set off from San Carlos late, which was unlike him. He always made sure to leave in time to make it back to camp before nightfall.

I wandered back to the lab. He'd turn up soon. I tried to go over my field notes, but I couldn't focus. The night wore on and no Guy. Could something have happened to him en route or perhaps in town? Might he be in hospital? Or was he delayed and chose to spend the night in a hotel? I realized I hadn't eaten all day. I didn't feel hungry, but I knew I should eat. I heaved myself out of my chair and went to the storeroom. I ate the rest of the gooseberry jam, scraping the jar clean with my forefinger, then took out the powdered eggs and marmalade to make a marmalade omelette. I also realized I was wearing the same clothes as the previous day. I went into the sleeping hut to change.

Something caught my eye as I unhooked the bag with my clothes from the rafter. The metal box containing our important papers, including my research, was askew, as if roughly shoved into its cubbyhole. I never left it that way. I drew it down and opened the lid as I held the lantern above it. All it contained was the plastic bag that held my passport, which I'd had to hand over to the National Guardsmen before we left the camp. All my research was gone, as was Guy's passport and our contract. A tide of nausea swept me. I turned to the shelf where Guy stored his things. His clothing was still there, but the plastic bag with his exercise books full of notes about the spiders and Tx2-6 extraction was not.

I ran to the specimen hut. The liter of Tx2-6 was gone, too. My head swam and my chest tightened. I had trouble drawing a breath. I hung on to a table and then in the light cast by the lantern on the tanks, I couldn't see any spiders. They were usually active at night. I went from tank to tank. They were all empty. He'd taken the spiders. He must've brought containers from town. Which meant . . . he'd planned this?

My legs quaked. I got myself to the lab and collapsed into the hammock. There had to be a logical reason why he'd taken everything, some scheme of his. He'd be back, laughing it off as usual. He couldn't have just . . . Or could he? Absolutely not. Above everything, Guy loved me. He loved me. I repeated those three words like a mantra. I fell into a stupor as night descended.

I slept fitfully through the night. As tendrils of light penetrated the darkness, I heard thuds around the camp. Footsteps. They didn't sound like Guy's, but my heart leapt. He was back! I scrambled to my feet and recognized the silhouetted outline of a cap. A National Guardsman. Something had happened to Guy. They'd come to tell me.

"Está acá!" he shouted before I knew it. She's here!

"Where's Guy?" I shouted in Spanish.

Several guardias jogged up and surrounded me.

"Doctora Rowena Aldus, you're under arrest," one said.

PART III

Pain streaked my chest. My eyes focused on a middle-aged man who seemed to be rubbing my sternum up and down with his knuckles, pressing hard. It was excruciating. The next thing I knew, a light blinded my eyes. I flinched. The glare left as suddenly as it came.

"She's come to," I heard the man say as he grabbed my wrist, underside up. He paused for a moment then dropped it. "She'll be alright. Just shock."

He got up. Shuffling footsteps, a metal clank, a rumble of deep voices. Silence. I sat up, remembering what had happened and calculating my current whereabouts. I'd been arrested. I was in a jail cell. Why, I didn't know. I got up from the narrow bed, crossed to the door slowly, feeling curiously leaden, and knocked on the metal door. I noticed a closed slot in the door at the height of my waist. I bent down and requested water. My voice emerged as a croak.

The slot in the door slid back and a woman's hand thrust a small tin cup of water through. I downed it in one go and requested another. After I'd gulped my third cup, I felt somewhat compos mentis. I took in my surroundings: a cot with a thin, stained mattress that bore the faint odor of ammonia, a coarse green blanket folded at its foot. A plastic bucket in a corner. I spread the blanket on top of the mattress and sat, wondering what on earth was going on. A few minutes later, a metallic jangle sounded outside my door. It swung open. The female guard entered and grabbed my arm. I complied without protest.

She marched me into an office and sat me in a chair facing the comandante. He picked up a small book in front of him, leafed through it, and then tossed it onto his desk with an air of disdain. My passport.

"Doctora Aldus, we received a complaint that you have committed an extremely serious offense. The denuncia alleges that you unlawfully used human subjects for scientific experimentation."

I felt an electric shock shoot through me but said nothing. What could I say? It was true.

"Since you are a foreign national and a flight risk, you will be detained until further notice. You may contact the British Embassy in Caracas."

That was the last thing I wanted. I had no intention of becoming one of those international causes célèbres, the object of some freedom-from-a-foreign-prison campaign. I didn't want any attention at all. I just wanted Guy.

"And your friend, Guy Westerphal, where is he?" I asked.

"He is not here."

"I wish to see Doctora Carlota Moreno," I said.

"I will call la doctora and notify her." He snapped his fingers, and I felt a grip on my upper arms like tight bracelets.

Back in the cell, I sat on the cot, my back against the wall, and waited for Carlota, my mind whirring.

Could the tribe have laid these charges against me? Possibly, but they hadn't shown any sign of disgruntlement. Perhaps they'd mentioned this wonder drug to fishermen in the river or some other outsider, who then had taken it upon themselves to report me. But to what end? A more likely scenario would've involved blackmailing me.

That left Guy. Had Arbillaga tipped him off about the complaint and he'd taken the research and the Tx2-6 for safekeeping? But that didn't make sense. He would've alerted me, and we both would've escaped. He couldn't have gone off alone. He needed me. We were a team.

Besides, it'd been his idea to use the tribe for trials. I'd gone along with it, so I was indeed guilty, but he had pushed it. A thought sparked. Guy must've gone to Puerto Ayacucho to intervene on my behalf with YOU, the director of the Institute of Scientific Research. One phone call from the institute and this would all be sorted. I just had to be patient. I breathed a sigh of relief. I'd stay in town until Guy got back and then we'd return to camp together.

Time ticked on. Where was Carlota? Had she abandoned me also? Despair gnawed at me.

The door opened and my guard entered. "You are free to go." I hesitated. Had I heard correctly? "La Doctora Moreno is waiting for you."

I followed the guard to the lobby where Carlota was seated on a bench. Her hair was now a too bright chestnut, which I found oddly uplifting. She sprang up when she saw me and seized my elbow.

"Come on before he changes his mind," she muttered in my ear. She guided me out the door. The intense early afternoon light pierced my eyes. I felt her propel me along to her car. "Get in." She didn't speak further until she'd pulled away from the Guardia Nacional station. "We have to move fast to get you out of the country tonight."

"What on earth are you talking about?"

"We're going to get you across the river to Colombia. I have your passport."

"I can't leave. I have to wait for Guy."

"Rowena, Guy had you arrested. He's gone."

I shook my head. "There's a logical explanation for all this. Guy will be able to sort it. You have to find . . ."

She cut in. "Guy is gone. For good. I made some inquiries after receiving the comandante's call. Guy flew to Puerto Ayacucho yesterday morning."

"He's probably gone to talk to the Institute on my behalf."

"You're not listening. The comandante told me that Guy filed the complaint against you. He's probably in Miami by now."

I slumped. "But . . . he couldn't have. They must have coerced him or . . . or . . . threatened him with something."

"Arbillaga told me himself. But luckily, all the comandante cares about is money. I convinced him that the complaint was all a lover's quarrel and had no merit."

"He believed that?"

"With the help of a generous sum. I know how he operates. He waits a day or two before notifying the prosecutor's office in Puerto Ayacucho of the pending case, which leaves ample time to make the charges disappear. Thankfully, we had your uncle's inheritance. We have to use the rest of it for a boat to pick you up tonight and take you to San Felipe. From there, you can get to Bogotá and fly home."

"My home is here," I bleated.

"Not anymore. One of Arbillaga's conditions for releasing you is that you leave Venezuela."

"I want to wait for Guy." I sounded like a petulant child.

"Rowena, he's not coming back. You have to leave the country." Carlota emphasized the words as if lecturing a dunce.

I fell silent as we pulled into Carlota's car port and entered her house. I didn't want to believe she was right, but of course she was telling me the truth. She instructed the maid to fix me a plate of chicken and rice as she escorted me to a spare bedroom. "Take a shower. I'll put some clean clothes on the bed. After you eat, we'll finish the arrangements."

"There's no other way?" I said.

"Do you want to spend the next decade in a Venezuelan prison?"

Under the shower's spray of lukewarm water, my head spun like a centrifuge. What had happened? Everything had been going unbelievably well, and then in the space of a few hours, my life had been smashed into smithereens. Had Guy really betrayed me? What was I going to do? Where would I go? I hadn't felt so bereft, so utterly alone and helpless, since my father died. I wouldn't even have Carlota for much longer.

When I sat at the table with Carlota where a meal awaited me, I had no energy to keep up a pretense. "My research and the Tx2-6 are gone," I admitted, staring at the food. "I've been an utter fool."

"He took advantage of you, Rowena. Probably from the start." Carlota rubbed my hand. "It happens. Eat."

"I'm actually not very hungry."

"You have a long journey ahead of you. You'll need your strength."

I ate a couple of forkfuls just to please her, then she insisted I get a few hours kip. I didn't think I could sleep but I must've dropped off.

It was night-time when she woke me and bundled me into her car. We drove out of town on the main road, the car's headlights carving bright cones out of the granite darkness. She turned onto a beaten track and parked. Reaching into the back seat, she handed me a rucksack. "There's a change of clothes in there, your passport and some money, Colombian pesos and American dollars. The front pocket has a flashlight. You'll need that for the walk into San Felipe."

On foot, we headed down to a sandy cove amid mangroves and waited on the riverbank. Stars sprinkled the sky like sugar crystals, but the Rio Negro lived up to its name, black as a bottomless abyss.

"Thank you, Carlota. I don't know . . ." I choked on a sob. She grasped my forearm in response.

"Get in touch when you're safe," she said. A long low whistle pierced the silence. "He's here." Carlota flashed her torch.

I embraced her and thanked her again.

"Good luck, Rowena. I will miss you."

I suspected I'd miss her more. A rowboat emerged from the inky atmosphere like a vision. I waded into the river and climbed into the dinghy. The boatman pushed us off and rowed into the blackness with clean, quiet slices, Charon ferrying me across the River Styx. I heard the faint sound of Carlota's car starting and felt forlorn.

A few minutes later, we docked on a muddy bank.

"San Felipe is a kilometer that way." The boatman pointed into the dark. "Follow the road. You'll see a house with a light in the front window. Knock at the door." As soon as I was out of the dinghy, he pulled the oars backward and was swallowed by the night.

I fished out the torch from the rucksack and found the dirt road. I walked at a steady clip, my senses on high alert for any predatory wildlife, animal or human, and soon came across buildings. A dog barked, startling me, then I saw a pinprick of light and picked up my pace. I walked up to the door of a whitewashed house and gently rapped. The door clicked open, and a teenage girl appeared in the crack holding a kerosene lamp.

"Pase." She opened the door just wide enough for me to slide through. I noticed she was in the latter stages of pregnancy.

I followed her down a narrow passage and out into a yard. She stopped in front of a doorway and gestured to a narrow room with a low wooden cot.

"Get some sleep. You'll be leaving early. Buenas noches."

I thanked her and sat on the bed. The mattress was hard and prickly, stuffed with straw. I lay back. Self-pity inundated me. My mother, wherever her soul had landed, must be getting a good laugh out of my misfortune, wagging her I-told-you-so finger. It turned out that she was right. No one ever really wanted me for me. I tossed and turned, wishing I had a coloring book and crayons. Finally, a rooster crowed somewhere, and I soon smelled wood smoke. The girl appeared at my door.

"Señora, I've prepared breakfast. You'll be leaving soon."

Dawn's pale light filtered through the trees as she showed me the outhouse with a toilet that was flushed with a bowl of water scooped out of a barrel. A sliver of soap and a threadbare towel sat folded neatly on a wooden chair. The water barrel also served as the bathing facility. I performed rudimentary ablutions and, shooing away hens running underfoot, returned to the kitchen, which was located under a roof at the back of the house and had cement benches and shelves. The girl was deftly shaping dough patties between her palms and tossing them onto a griddle over a fire.

"Buenos días," I said.

A smile displayed her front teeth, which were bordered by gold, and she returned the greeting. She pointed at a table covered with a plastic tablecloth and wiped her hands on the apron stretched across her ballooning belly. I sat and she set before me a plate of arepas, made Colombian style with wheat flour instead of cornmeal as in Venezuela, scrambled eggs and black beans. I ate as much as I could, not wanting to waste the meal, but I wasn't very hungry. She brought me a cup of black coffee. I ladled sugar into it and stirred.

"Osvaldo is loading the truck now. He'll drop you in Inírida. You can get a bus or plane to Bogotá from there."

I knew from maps that Inírida was a fairly large town, bigger than

San Carlos. "How far is it?"

"Two hundred and forty kilometers, but it's paved the whole way."

Four to five hours journey, depending on road conditions. Paved didn't mean a whole lot in a region that caught torrential rains half the year. I carried my empty plate and cup to the sink, a plastic tub fed by a garden hose that was connected to a tap in the yard and draped over the kitchen half-wall.

A thought occurred to me. "Would it be possible to stay a while in San Felipe? I could rent a room from someone."

A pained look crossed her face. "It would be very dangerous."

I was baffled as to her meaning. "Because of the Venezuelan Guardia Nacional?"

"No, la guerrilla. They come to town sometimes. If they see a foreigner . . ."

"Señora, are you ready to go?" A man stood in the threshold between the house and kitchen. Judging by the looseness of his jowls, he looked quite a bit older than the girl and had a paunch as big as her pregnant stomach.

"Lista," I said. Ready.

A battered pickup truck was parked at the side of the house, which probably meant the couple was relatively well off in this remote pocket, perhaps from their sideline of providing a waystation to Venezuelan fugitives. Maybe money was the reason why the girl had married him. The truck bed was covered with a tarp, whose bumpy surface hinted at plenty of goods underneath that I presumed he was going to sell in town.

Osvaldo was already behind the steering wheel. I climbed in beside him. With a wave to the girl, we were off. In two minutes, San Felipe was well behind us. We rocketed along a narrow strip of asphalt, its borders laced with jungle, the wind a dull roar through Osvaldo's open window.

Plagued by the unknown ahead of me, I hadn't any appetite for conversation. Neither, thankfully, did Osvaldo. For too many years to count, my life had been as predictable as the time of sunrise and sunset year-round on the Equator. Undoubtedly, monotony was accompanied by a certain safety and comfort, but it also flattened life to its most elemental. Perhaps that's why I had fallen so hard for Guy. He had spiced up my life, made it exciting, promising, something I hadn't been able to do except through the artificial means of yopo. Now I had no idea what was to happen in an hour's time, let alone the following day. I leaned my head back and let myself be lulled by the rhythm of the road. At least, I was in motion. It was better than being stationary. And I had money. I could stay in Inírida, living on the cheap, until I figured out what to do next.

Comforted by having at least a small step mapped out and having barely slept the night before, I fell into a light sleep.

I started at the jerk of a downshift and raised my head to see three oil barrels barricading the road ahead of us. Osvaldo swore under his breath.

"Just do what they say," he said.

I hadn't the foggiest whom he was referring to. So far no one had made themselves visible. But as Osvaldo halted, a band of men swarmed out of the jungle and surrounded the truck, levelling assault rifles at us. They wore handkerchiefs tied around their faces, one wore a balaclava and another a T-shirt wrapped around his head leaving only a strip for his eyes.

One of them approached Osvaldo's window. "Compañero, where are you going?"

"Inírida, to the market."

He peered at me for a moment. "¿Quién es?"

"A passenger. I'm taking her to the bus station."

He studied me a moment longer, as if deciding something, then beckoned. "Out of the truck."

I glanced at Osvaldo, who almost imperceptibly lifted his chin in a nod. My heart hammering, I got out. The man told me to put my hands on my head then reached in and grabbed my rucksack from the front seat.

Another man patted me down whilst the first rifled through my bag. Another had lifted the tarp over the truck bed and was inspecting the merchandise. The one with my rucksack found my passport. He crossed to the man who seemed to be the leader and showed it to him. They conferred for a second, then the leader looked at me.

"You're coming with us," he said.

I shot a beseeching look at Osvaldo, who remained impassive, clenching the steering wheel. Something hard poked me in the back, making me stagger forward past the oil drums to a pickup truck with its rear gate down.

"Get in," someone ordered. I climbed into the truck bed, which was loaded with bulging burlap sacks. An empty sack was shoved over my head, and my arms were pulled behind my back and tied so tight that the rope cut into my wrists. The sack, full of bits of straw and dust that scratched my face, made it hard to breathe.

My mood sank. I'd been taken hostage by highwaymen. They had stumbled on the jackpot of a European foreigner, which to them meant money. Little did they know, no one was going to pay any ransom to rescue me, nor did I have access to a bank account. All that I possessed in the world was in my rucksack.

We soon got going. As the truck sped along, every hump in the road rattled my bones, and I leaned against the sacks for support. I assumed we were on a dirt track through the jungle. The bag on my head was stifling, and perspiration dripped into my eyes, stinging them. I pressed them shut and took shallow breaths to conserve air.

The journey seemed interminable. At times we slowed to a crawl, and the truck swung wildly from side to side, indicating we were travelling on a stretch of road cratered with potholes. We were going deeper into the rainforest. Light seeped through the weave of the sack and the heat and humidity intensified. It must be nearing midday. My throat scraped with thirst. I swallowed as much as I could to moisten it, but I didn't have much liquid left in me. I grew dizzy.

We finally came to a complete stop. Vehicle doors opened and closed, several at once. Voices rumbled. I strained to listen, but they were too far away. The truck bed bounced with the weight of people jumping in and unloading the cargo. Then my upper arms were seized on each side. I was hauled to my feet, marched to the tip of the truck bed and ordered to jump. I hesitated and hands pushed my upper back. I crashed to the ground in a heap.

"Get her up! Give her some water!" An authoritative voice, a woman's.

I was pulled to my feet and my hood was removed. I gasped to get as much air as I could. Everything was a blur then my vision focused. People in olive-green fatigues. The army. I was rescued! A soldier held a canteen to my lips, and I gulped the water. It was warm and tasted slightly rank, but it was wet. The overflow splashed down my chin and neck.

After I finished drinking, I surveyed the scene. My captors, muscular young men, formed a chain to unload the truck. The soldiers, assault rifles hanging from their shoulders like extra appendages, were pouring the rice and beans from the sacks into smaller bags. They tied the tops in a knot and stuffed them into large rucksacks. What on earth . . .?

I looked for the woman who seemed to be in charge. She was talking with one of my kidnappers. My rucksack was at her feet, and she was examining something. My passport. My shoulders ached from being pulled back. I shifted them with difficulty. Why weren't they cutting the ties off my hands? What was taking so long? I was debating on calling out to the woman when I spotted the soldiers' footwear.

They weren't wearing military-issue lace-up boots. They wore black, knee-high rubber boots, wellies. These weren't soldiers in the Colombian army. They were guerrillas in El Frente Armado de Liberación Colombiana, the Colombian Armed Liberation Front, the FALC. And I wasn't being rescued. I was being sold to the guerrillas by the bandits. I closed my eyes as despondence overcame me. The FALC were notorious for keeping hostages for years deep in the jungle. If they were deemed unworthy of keeping around, they were shot.

After the truck was unloaded, my captors left. I was moved to the shade and told to sit. A guerrilla, maybe fifteen years old judging by the dark peach fuzz on his upper lip, was assigned to guard me. He freed my hands and gave me a hunk of stale bread to eat and more water. This time I ate and drank everything. I had no idea when I'd eat next. I asked him where they were going. He told me to shut up. I noticed him worrying a tooth with his tongue and occasionally sucking in his jaw.

"Toothache?" I said.

He answered with a glare. After all the sacks of food brought by the robbers were redistributed, the insurgents sat under trees, ate and rested.

The leader strutted up to me and crouched, asking if I spoke Spanish. I nodded. She said her name was Tania. "What are you doing in Colombia?"

I thought quickly. I couldn't say I had escaped from Venezuela, or they could turn me in for money. "Scientific research. I study the medicinal properties of tropical flora and fauna. I should warn you, the British government doesn't pay ransom for hostages."

She gave a half-smile. "That's what they all say publicly. Do as you're told, and you won't be harmed. Get some sleep, if you can. You'll need it." She straightened and left me.

At dusk, Tania bellowed an order to break camp. The soldiers stood and slung on heavy packs laden with the small bags of rice and beans and other goods. After forming a column, we marched into the jungle. My eyes gradually became accustomed to the lack of light, but I couldn't see much.

"Keep your eyes on the knapsack in front of you and you'll be okay," my minder said as he bound my wrists with a rope.

The pace was rapid, and everyone was expected to keep up. Of course, they were both well used to this physical exertion and much younger than I. After some hours, my feet were rubbed raw in my shoes, my muscles ached, my clothing soaked with sweat. Every step became an exercise in pain. I begged to rest, to drink water. But all I got from my handler was a sharp prod of the rifle, reminding me who held the power. I stumbled a couple of times when my feet refused to keep working. A jab in the ribs got them moving again. With every step of agony, I blamed Guy, but the physical torment grew to the point that it blocked all thought. Small mercies, indeed.

Close to daylight, we halted, bivouacking under nylon tarps the guerrillas expertly strung up between trees. I collapsed next to a base of exposed roots and managed to shuck off my boots with my hands still tied at the wrist. My minder showed no intention of untying my hands. My socks were saturated with blood. I peeled them off carefully. My feet were a pulpy mess. I visually searched the brush as light sifted through the sieve of the tree canopy. I spotted what I needed just beyond the tarped area.

I turned to my guard. "I need some of those leaves over there. Shapumvilla. They stop bleeding." He stared at me. "Please, I need them for my feet."

"You know jungle medicine?"

This was a chance to win a friend. "Yes. Do you want something for that toothache?"

He hesitated. I could see by the bulge in his cheek that his tongue was rubbing his bad molar. He went over to the group. Most were eating. Some were already snoring.

My minder returned and pointed his rifle toward the forest. "Hurry. Make any move and I'll shoot."

We dove into the forest and awkwardly, as my wrists were tied, I pulled off as many leaves as I could hold in my hands. I pulled off a handful of shapumvilla leaves. Then I looked around. Please, let there be a spilanthes plant. If there wasn't, I would give him some shapumvilla. A lot of medicinal plants had numerous uses. Even if it didn't work, the placebo effect might. I walked farther in, my eyes hunting for the yellow flower.

"Vamos. We can't take too long," my guard said.

Reluctantly, I turned then I spotted a flash of color. I stopped and pointed. "Over there."

He glanced in the direction of the camp. "We've already spent too much time."

"That's the flower."

His face clenched with pain. "Hurry then."

I found the plant and told the guard to pluck off all the blooms, which he did, stuffing them in his jacket pocket. "Chew a little at a time, on the side with the bad tooth." I told him.

He did so and motioned me back to camp. Another guerrilla came up to him. "Where the fuck were you?"

"She took a long time taking a shit."

I assumed he lied because he didn't want to give the impression that he was granting me favors. I cleaned my feet with water as best I could and covered them with the shapumvilla leaves. They felt better instantly. I was given a plate of cold rice and beans. As the sun rose, the camp fell quiet with exhaustion. I sank into a deep sleep, ignoring the pain of my cuffed wrists, awakening at one point to the plinking of rain into pots set out to catch water then drifting back off.

In the afternoon, my guard wakened me with a rough shake. After eating leftover beans and bitter black coffee brewed with rainwater, we broke camp and set off trudging through boot-sticking mud, the shapumvilla leaves encasing my feet under my socks. My muscles had stiffened during sleep and screamed with every step. They gradually loosened. It was the same tortuous routine as the previous day. When we broke briefly at midnight, I asked my guard his name.

"Antonio," he said.

Not his real name, of course. Guerrillas adopted noms de guerre to disguise their identity and protect their families from retribution. "How's the tooth?"

He nodded. It was too much to expect a display of gratitude, I supposed.

The rest was brief, then we resumed the godforsaken march up the side of a mountain. Why would anyone sign up for this?

It started to rain when we reached the ridge, a sudden deluge of fat drops. We plodded on, getting drenched as we were out of the protection of the jungle canopy. The guerrillas opened their canteens to catch the water. The rain soon passed, or we passed it, and the air turned into a steam bath. At one point, someone shouted, and everyone dove into the vegetation beside the track. My guard pulled me along with him. The thwop-thwop of a helicopter sounded above us.

"The Army," Antonio said.

I briefly wondered whether I should leap out of the brush and wave my arms, but what good would that do? The helicopter couldn't land on a mountain ridge. The guerrillas would gun me down. I stayed put. When we could no longer hear the aircraft, we resumed our trek, which soon turned into a steep descent into the valley on the other side of the ridge. I slipped twice on the muddy trail and landed with a thud on my bum. I added backache to my litany of pains. Finally, we reached the valley floor, and soon the scent of burning wood pricked my nostrils. Civilization was near. I'd never felt so grateful for anything in all my life.

The entire column seemed to feel similarly. Everyone picked up their pace, finding that last bit of strength to get home, like horses when they know they're close to their stable. We entered a clearing populated with wooden buildings, and I was shunted into a hut that contained a camp bed. I barely registered the click of a padlock on the door as I collapsed on the bed. After sleeping on the ground, a piece of canvas strung over a wooden frame seemed deluxe indeed. Everything hurt but fatigue overpowered pain. It seemed that I had only slept ten minutes when Antonio woke me up with an aluminum dish of rice, beans, boiled yuca and a mug of black coffee.

"We're leaving soon."

I groaned inwardly. Another death march.

He and a comrade escorted me about two kilometers along a worn path to a riverbank where a long wooden boat with a roof over most of its length waited. They ushered me on board into the middle of a cluster of metal drums, which contained kerosene judging by the smell, and seated me on the floor with my hands and feet tied. A large heavy tarp was thrown over the lot and a rope tied around the barrels to prevent movement. The overpowering odor in the airless space soon gave me a migraine, but at least I wasn't walking.

I was left to my own thoughts. I leaned back and tried to remember my maps of Colombia's Amazon basin. Which river could this be? I couldn't summon anything.

Inevitably, my mind drifted to Guy. I wondered where he was, what he was doing. I realized I actually knew next to nothing about him, only the little he'd chosen to tell me. I had no independent corroboration of anything he'd said. Had he planned to steal my research from the start? Or at some later point, after he had seen it would be easy for him to do so? The relentless questions about the spiders, their diet and habitat, and then about the Tx2-6 extraction. The exercise books of his notes. The trips to town. All part of his plan, undoubtedly. Why had I gone along with him so blindly? What had I not seen? I'd vetted him on the internet, although I'd only found one profile on that business website. I recalled that when he told me about himself at dinner, it was almost as if he were reciting directly from his online CV. It was too perfect.

His jibber-jabber about the conservation station. He'd played into my dream, correctly surmising that was the key to unlocking my trust. That was probably the moment that I fully opened to him. Hindsight made everything look as clear as a mountain stream.

We stopped at a couple of ports during the day. There was a lot of shouting, thunks of cargo being loaded, the grating of boxes being pushed around on the wooden deck. Antonio gave me an arepa and water and took me to a smelly toilet. I questioned him about where we were going. It was an unsettling feeling, being completely powerless over my own fate.

"Another camp. It's a while downriver yet." His vagueness was annoying.

I asked if I could sit outside the tarp to get fresh air, but he shook his head. "Too risky." I supposed that meant there was other traffic on the river, possibly police of some sort.

I took advantage of the time to rest and tried to empty my mind. Finally, we seemed to be slowing and the tarp was pulled back from the drums. We'd arrived.

Antonio helped me to my feet as we putted to shore. Big sections of leafy brush slid back to expose a small beach where the boat maneuvered to a position parallel to the bank. Two guerrillas appeared and waited for the boat hand to slide off the gangway, which they positioned in the sand. We proceeded ashore, where several men in shorts and flip-flops, their wide cheekbones indicating indigenous heritage, several with their calves and shins red and raw as if they'd been scrubbed with a hard bristle brush, waited with dollies. Campesinos not guerrillas. They didn't even glance at me as they crowded onto the boat and rolled the drums down the gangway, tying them onto the dollies, which they pushed down a path into the forest. I could see the earth was packed and deeply rutted, which told me heavy cargo regularly travelled the track.

The pieces clicked into place. There was one jungle industry that required campesinos and huge quantities of kerosene. The manufacture of cocaine.

I congratulated myself. I was thinking clearly again, more like my old self. The boat journey had been unnerving in that I didn't know where I was going, but it had been a day's rest.

After conferring with a guerrilla from this camp, Antonio turned me over to his custody. My new guard marched me in a direction opposite to where the men had taken the drums and, within minutes, we reached a clearing, dim due to the overhead netting tied to trees and twined with dark green leaves — camouflage against Army helicopters, I presumed.

We halted outside a wooden hut, where another guerrilla stood sentry. My guard told me to wait, and he went inside. I seized the moment to take stock of the place. The camp seemed larger than the previous one. Guerrillas were cleaning and oiling their rifles. Some kicked a football around. A couple of women laughed as they carried a wooden box across the camp between them. The atmosphere seemed easy.

The door opened. "Comandante Omar will see you," the guard said.

He prodded me into a hut where a stocky man, his beard salted with specks of white, wiped his face with a hand towel. He tossed it over a shoulder as the guard indicated that I should take a wooden chair in front of the desk where Omar sat. I could see my passport in front of him. Behind him, a sun-faded picture of Fidel Castro hung on the wall, cigar clamped between his teeth. It looked like it had been cut out of a magazine.

I sat with a ramrod back and chin up to show him I was not

intimidated. "Buenas tardes, Comandante. I wish to know when I'm being released."

He let a full second pass before answering, to show who was boss, I thought. "I was told that you know about jungle medicine."

"Yes."

"We have several compañeros who are sick, and we're low on medical supplies. I'd like you to take a look at them, see what you can do."

Why should I do anything for a band of thugs? I almost refused, but then I realized I had more to gain through acquiescence, for now at least. "Of course, comandante."

He opened his right-hand drawer and tossed my passport in it, which I committed to memory. After he issued orders conditioned with threats — "If you try to escape, we'll shoot you on sight," "You make life easy for us, we'll make life easy for you," and so forth — I was walked over to a long wooden hut. It was the sick bay. Three young men lay on stretcher beds. I asked each of them their symptoms. One had amoebic dysentery, another was covered in red pustules, possibly an allergic reaction, and another was sweating and shaking with a high fever, and his skin looked jaundiced. It could be malaria, hepatitis or even yellow fever.

"Was he on antimalarials?" I asked the woman who seemed to be acting as nurse.

"We've run out here, but he came from the interior. I don't know what they do at that camp."

"Do you not have a medic?"

"He was killed, and the doctor we used in town has moved away."

I did my best to speak with medical authority, although I had nothing of the sort. "Keep them all cool with compresses and give them all plenty of water, so they don't get dehydrated. It's very important." I turned to my escort. "I'll need to go out and look for plants in the forest in the morning."

"I'll check with the comandante."

He took me to a small, windowless wooden hut surrounded by a wire fence like an animal pen. They obviously were used to holding hostages here. The hut had just enough room for a camp bed, small table and chair. A bucket in the corner by the door served as a toilet. As with the previous hut, I was locked in with a padlock.

I lay down on the bed and assessed my situation. This camp had river access, boats coming and going. The woman mentioned a doctor "in town" so there must be a settlement of some size not too far away. My best hope for escape would be by water. Overland through deep jungle would be well-nigh impossible. I needed to remain here, so it was crucial that I manage to improve the three patients' conditions.

The next morning after breakfast and a quick check on the patients, I went on a foraging expedition into jungle accompanied by two guards. I managed to gather an assortment of leaves and barks that I needed and others that I might need in the future, collecting them in a sack I had found in the clinic. I felt relaxed for the first time since my arrest as I wandered in the dappled light immersed in the symphony of birds and monkeys. For just that little while, I was able to forget I was captive.

When I returned, I covered the man's rash with the red latex of the sangre de grado tree and ground up bark of the chinchona tree to make quinine for the fever patient. For the man with dysentery, I gave him lapacho leaves to alleviate pain in his stomach and the cola de ratón plant to help him keep water and food down. I worked at a small bench off to the side, grinding barks and labelling leaves to start forming a medicine cabinet.

Around midday, Comandante Omar popped in and spoke to the three patients. Then he approached me.

"It appears you know your stuff. They say they're feeling better."

"It'll take a few days. I'm trying to stabilize the dysentery patient, but he needs metronidazole. It's really the only thing that kills the parasites. And antimalarials are a must."

"The Army has blocked our supply route, that's why we're running low. I'll work on it."

"I need to collect a lot more plants to build up a good stock of medicines."

He nodded. "Muy bien. I'll have two guards accompany you." As he turned to go, I made a last pitch. "Comandante, the patients need protein: eggs, broth made with meat, chicken, fish."

He glared at me, incensed at my telling him what to do but I wanted him to feel my small authority. He left, and I exhaled. I had passed the initial test.

The following day, bowls of fish broth were delivered to the infirmary. The guerrillas had evidently been assigned to go fishing. It was an encouraging sign that the comandante was taking me seriously.

My days soon settled into a routine. Every morning, I'd assess how patients did overnight, then go out plant-hunting in the jungle for a couple hours in different directions so I could gather the widest variety of plants, trying to commit their locations to memory as my request for pencil and paper had been refused. I kept a sharp lookout for a road or sign of human presence, but never detected anything. We were deep in the forest, as I had presumed, which confirmed the river as my best means of escape. My guards were always careful to steer me away from taking an easterly direction, standing in front of me and silently pointing their weapons the opposite way. I deduced it must be the location of the coca processing operation.

I spent the rest of the day in the infirmary, treating the steady stream of patients, pulverizing barks and branches, macerating leaves and blooms. It kept me busy, for which I was grateful. Without the infirmary, I'd be confined to the small hut, days long with unrelenting boredom and the ceaseless labyrinth of rumination.

During the solitary nights, however, I fell into that mental maze. How could Guy have betrayed me? Had he ever loved me, felt passion for me, even the tiniest smidgen? Long after the camp went to sleep at nightfall, except for the guards who circled the perimeter at all times, I'd lie awake and parse every minute of my time with him until I fell into exhausted sleep.

I saw how naïve I'd been from the get-go, how I'd so willingly fallen into his trap because I'd wanted to believe him. I had mistaken his lies for promises, his promises for intent. I'd seen his evident love for his daughter and claimed it as mine, as the paternal protection that I'd lost with my own father's early demise. Guy must've been laughing at me from the start, marvelling in his good fortune that he'd found such a ready victim. Straight away, he'd seen my vulnerabilities, my severe loneliness, my dashed dreams, and he'd pounced on them, inflating them to the wildest possible extent. A pre-eminent Amazon global research station. A rebel pharmaceutical movement. He'd clearly done his research before "bumping into me" in Puerto Ayacucho. I felt sure he'd paid YOU and/or the comandante to have me brought in on some pretext.

Then after establishing himself in my camp, Guy took control of it, and I, eager to please, so thankful for any scrap of attention, had let him. He pushed me incessantly to finish the research whilst establishing his own contacts with the tribe and the comandante, buying their allegiance with fancy meals and trinkets, all the time isolating me from my only friend Carlota. The incident with the letter. I supposed I had an inkling that something was awry, but I couldn't allow that hurtful thought to surface, so I shoved it deep down, made excuses for him. I had no such barrier now. The only reason that I could see for his hiding the letter is that it promised me money, and he wanted me to be totally dependent upon him to cement his control.

I castigated myself for being such a bloody fool, for actually believing that a man could ever want me for me. Even my father had used me as an excuse to flee the house. "She needs fresh air and exercise," he'd say to my mother, who'd glower at me as if it were my fault Dad wanted to take away her small servant, her vessel to fill with abuse, for the day. Was there ever a purpose in human relationship beyond utility? Was selfish interest a pre-requisite of all of mankind's interaction?

But why had Guy gone to the extent of the whirlwind romance? He could've presented a deal without using my heart as collateral. Perhaps, I thought, he really did fall in love with me. Just a bit. We'd shared pleasant times, laughed at private jokes, enjoyed each other's company. Maybe he'd done a runner because he couldn't bear to say goodbye to me. He knew he'd crumble if he told me he was leaving because he loved me. It was a comforting thought that led to elaborate fantasies of our reunion where he'd admit to his mistake, declare his undying love for me and beg me for forgiveness. I'd forgive him and we'd live happily ever after. Gradually, I overcame the sticky puddle of self-censure and woe-is-me pity. I managed to bury the hard chip of bitterness, and I was left with the storybook fantasy that Guy had loved me, that something had happened during his trip into town that day, perhaps the comandante had threatened to arrest Guy, too, but he fled in time, or managed to escape. Guy would've sprung me from jail eventually. This foolish reverie, which blithely ignored all facts and rationality, was nevertheless the only thing I had to hang on to.

With my mind keeping me awake well into many nights, I'd hear noise from the riverbank every so often. Without the daily bustle of the camp, sound carried. The growl of voices, the knock of an engine. Boats arriving and departing soon after, surely connected to the coca operation, collections of processed material and deliveries of prime materials. I timed the nocturnal arrivals. The boats docked once every seven or eight days.

One day, I found a small screwdriver, the type used to repair eyeglasses, on the floor of the infirmary, undoubtedly dropped by a recent, spectacle-wearing patient. He'd come in from the jungle with a sore lump on his leg caused by caterpillar larvae hatching under his skin, not an uncommon ailment. I immediately scooped up the tiny tool and deposited it in the gusset of my underpants to avoid detection from the pat-down search when I left the infirmary at night.

I used it to dig out a small spyhole in a knot on the edge of a wooden plank near the floor. Squatting, I'd put my eye to it and take in the nightly goings-on. I noticed a curious thing. Metal drums would sometimes be brought to Comandante Omar's hut and rolled inside. I wondered what they contained. Weapons, probably. They had plenty of arms but were scant on basic medicines. Human capital was worth less than their precious bullets. When too many had died, they'd simply pressgang more poor, rural youths into joining their ranks. I also noticed other arrivals and departures from Omar's hut—those of a female guerrilla who looked barely out of her teens.

I was careful not to ask many questions about the camp lest I arouse suspicions, but I observed and listened keenly, piecing together bits and pieces of information like a jigsaw. The camp, I concluded, was a transit point. Guerrillas came and went, sometimes arriving by boat, other times overland to pick up supplies that were shipped in — munitions, food, and household items like soap and scrub brushes — and transport them back to their jungle bivouacs. Sometimes guerrillas had to wait a couple days for their cargoes, so they were able to relax in the meantime.

That was also why the camp had an infirmary. Ill or injured guerrillas would arrive from the interior, sometimes carried on a litter through the jungle for several days. More than once, they were dead on arrival or succumbed soon afterward. When the FALC had had a friendly doctor, they'd be taken by boat to the town, but now they stayed in the sick bay to be treated by me with my crude remedies.

My reputation as a healer soon spread. The rebel soldiers would come to the sick bay with all manner of complaints. I'd give them matico leaf tea for coughs and colds, jaborandi for gonorrhea, which they'd bring back after visits home, tawari bark to fight infected toenails and wounds, lapacho leaves for menstrual pain. When they set out for lengthy journeys inland, I handed them supplies of achiote to use as an insect repellent, as well as suma, an energizer.

Months flowed by like a river. I tried to stay current with the passage of time by keeping a calendar and periodically asking patients what month and day it was — some didn't know either — but then I gave up. What was the point? I had no discernible future, just the present.

I gradually built a bridge of trust with the rank-and-file guerrillas. They'd tell me snippets of camp gossip, anecdotes about their lives before joining the FALC, and bring me bits-and-bobs that I could use. Baskets and woven pouches for the medicines. A piece of rope that I fashioned into a strap for my plant sack so I could wear it across my body. Chips of soap and small quantities of toothpaste or shampoo. A dog-eared romance novel with its covers torn off that I devoured. We didn't have much in camp, me especially, so I made good use of anything that I could cadge or was given.

They started to call me "doctora," a contravention of their Marxist doctrine of equality that dictated everyone was a "compañero," or "camarada." It was a sign that they respected me, but I was still very much a prisoner. I was not allowed to circulate in the camp. My movements were limited to going between my hut and the infirmary, accompanied by a guard, and two guards when I went into the forest scouting for plants, the only times I felt some semblance of freedom. Still, I contented myself with the thought that my situation could be a lot worse.

One night I was engaging in a fantasy about spurning Guy's plea for forgiveness and making my formula a huge success on my own and then taking him back, when a massive boom bolted me out of bed. My first thought was the Army. My spirits skyrocketed. I was going to be rescued! A volley of chaotic shouts ensued. I peeked through the spyhole, hoping to spot a passing soldier I could appeal to for aid. But in the moonlit darkness, all I could detect were flitting silhouettes and the stampede of running boots toward the eastern end of camp. I saw the woman guerrilla slip out of Omar's hut, then the comandante emerged from his hut, buckling his belt.

"Auxilio!" I called several times. Help!

No one paid any attention. Then someone was outside fumbling with the padlock. I stood ready. The door swung open.

"Doctora, venga." Come. To my disappointment, a guerrilla stood in the threshold, not a soldier. I smelled smoke, more acrid than burning wood. Fuel. The coca lab had exploded.

He led me towards the inlet where the boats docked, and I heard a horrendous screech. The guerrillas had formed a human chain from the river down the trail that led to the coca lab. One person was filling containers with water and passing them to the next person, creating a line of swinging arms and bodies. My escort pointed to the source of the screams.

A teenage boy lay on the ground, the skin of his face, chest and arms peeled to the red of raw flesh. Pangs of horror rattled me as I ran over. Two campesinos were nearby. One man was pressing his head as blood trickled down his face. The other was holding his head in his hands but looked unscathed. The burnt boy was in agony. He needed morphine and a hospital, neither of which were available. I knew what might work instead of morphine. I addressed the workers.

"The coca, where is it?"

The unhurt one pointed to a mound of yellowish-brown goo sitting on a black plastic sheet near them. They'd saved it, I assumed. Using the cups of both hands, I scooped up the paste.

"Let's get the boy to the infirmary and I'll look at your wounds too. What's his name?"

"Ismael. He's Josue's nephew."

"And your name?"

"Ezekiel."

Between us, we carried the boy to the infirmary and laid him on a bed. Cocaine hydrochloride was actually one of the most effective topical anesthetics known to man, but all I had was raw coca paste and no hydrochloride. The only liquid on hand was the water I boiled for twenty minutes every day for treating wounds and drinking.

I grabbed all available bandages, which weren't many, and tossed a towel to Ezekiel, instructing him to rip it into strips. I poured a cup of some purified water, added a pinch of the coca paste, measuring by eye as I had no proper measuring tool. Too much and he'd overdose. Not enough and it would have null effect. After a vigorous mixing, the coca solid dissolved. I soaked the bandages in the solution and gently placed them over the burnt area. The boy, who'd been slipping in and out of consciousness, blacked out due to pain shutting down his brain or easing from the coca. Either way, we all felt relief.

I turned to Josue's injured scalp. He'd banged it on a bench as he fell. It was a superficial scrape, but heads wounds bled a lot. As I was cleaning it, Omar stalked in, his face and clothing streaked with soot and sweat, his face set with fury. His eyes alighted on the remains of the coca paste.

"That was not yours to take."

I wasn't going to let him intimidate me. "I did what I had to do, and it worked." I gestured to the unconscious boy.

"You should have used something else."

"Nothing except morphine that can relieve this level of pain." I felt a burst of rage. "What's a boy doing working here anyway?"

Omar shot me a thunderous look. "We'll continue this discussion in the morning." He left. An unsettled silence descended.

"Gracias, doctora," Josue whispered. "The boy is my sister's. It was his first night working with us."

"What happened?"

The workers glanced at each other, then Ezekiel pushed back a grimy, fraying baseball hat on his head and scratched his hairline.

"We were diluting the acid. Ismael poured water into the barrel, and it boiled up in his face. He jumped back and the stick he was using to stir the acid knocked over the barrel. It spilled on him. Josue was taking break, smoking a cigarette. He ran to help his nephew and must've tossed the cigarette into some kerosene on the ground. It caught fire."

"I told him to do it the other way," Josue said.

I nodded. "Acid to the water."

"He got it mixed up. He's fifteen," Ezekiel said.

"Do you usually work so late at night?"

"Only when we have a shipment to make. We were behind because the leaf delivery was late. That's why I brought the boy to help," Josue said.

"The son of a bitch is going to take the cost of the coca out of our pay," Ezekiel said.

Josue nodded.

"How does he pay you?" I asked.

"Cash," Ezekiel said.

"How does he get that?"

"It comes in barrels on the boats. That's how he pays everyone, the farmers, the boats, us."

The drums I'd seen rolled to Omar's hut.

A guerrilla entered to stand guard over us. We could no longer talk, which was unfortunate. I wanted to ask them about nearby towns. Ezekiel left to survey the state of the lab. I told my guard that I'd have to stay in the infirmary the rest of the night in case the boy or his uncle woke up. He nodded and I lay down in an empty bed, but I got little sleep.

The next morning, I requested to see the comandante. He sent for me an hour later. As I was ushered into his office, I noticed a door off to the side, which I hadn't seen on my first visit. That must be his bedroom and storage for the money barrels.

"Comandante, the boy needs to get to a hospital as soon as possible. I can't do much for him. His burns are third-degree. He needs skin grafts or he'll die. Can you get a boat here?"

"I'll see what I can do. From now on, you are not permitted to touch anything beyond what is in the infirmary. Understood?"

"Bien," I said. "And one more thing, I'd like to move into the room off the infirmary. The patients need round-the-clock care. There have been times when they've suffered setbacks overnight because no one was there to tend to them. You can still lock me in at night."

Omar studied me for a moment, then nodded. "De acuerdo."

I left the commandant's office feeling as if I'd won a concession. I had the guard accompany me directly to my hut and I moved my meager belongings to the more spacious infirmary.

The burnt boy and his uncle were taken away on a boat the following morning and I never saw them again. I often wondered how they fared, whether the FALC ever gave them any compensation for their injuries. I doubted it. I didn't see Ezekiel again either.

I liked living in the infirmary. It relieved my long nights of loneliness and boredom. I sat and talked with the patients, listened to their tales of nightmares and paranoia after skirmishes with the army, depression at being far from family, romantic troubles. If I felt like being alone, I busied myself in a corner with purpose, making up powders, boiling water, rolling bandages.

Nursing people back to health delivered fast results, unlike the glacial, tedious pace of science. I liked being looked up to, being sought for advice, but I couldn't let myself grow complacent, trust them as I had trusted Guy. With Guy, I didn't know who he was really, but I did know who the FALC was, a sociopathic band of narcotrafficking kidnappers, and my destiny was subject to their whims.

One evening, just after nightfall, a young woman showed up at the door. I recognized her as Comandante Omar's paramour. Her face was drawn, and purpled crescents underlined her eyes.

"Doctora, I need your help," she said in a low voice.

I immediately suspected it had something to do with female troubles and showed her to my "consulting room" off the infirmary. I asked her name. It was Frida.

"I think I'm pregnant," she blurted. "I'm late, almost four weeks, and I'm never late. Do you have something to . . .?"

"Omar?"

She looked at me startled.

"Don't worry. Your secret is safe with me, but I'm sure the whole camp knows about your relationship."

"If he finds out, he'll transfer me far away." She scratched the back of her left hand, which I noticed looked raw. "He'd never recognize the child. It's better just to . . ." Her voice trailed off, and I nodded.

I knew of a yellow-flowering plant called ruda that served as an abortifacient, but I hadn't seen it in my excursions around camp. Then again, I'd had no call for it thus far. It was cultivated all over the world and my mother had grown it in her garden, selling its oil to stimulate uterine contractions. I'd seen it in the village in Venezuela, so I thought I could likely locate it. I'd have to bring my one pair of surgical gloves, which I washed repeatedly, as its leaves could cause dermatitis.

"I don't have what I need. I'll have to go out and look for it," I said. "Come back this time tomorrow."

The following morning, I advised the guards that I needed to go deeper into the forest to find new plants. My escorts were hardly overjoyed at the prospect, but they knew whatever I collected helped everyone. I was also a model prisoner, never doing anything to arouse their suspicions. They stood well behind me with their guns, machetes in fringed leather sheaths hanging from their belts, gossiping in low voices. They'd look up and swivel their heads to check on me every now and then. As long as I stayed within sight, they gave me free rein.

I went off in a direction I hadn't yet explored because of its thick undergrowth. As I searched the bushes, I detected a flash of neon color. I painstakingly moved a large leaf and gasped. A diminutive frog gazed back at me with its overlarge eyes. About two inches long, neon yellow, with three toes, the middle one larger than those flanking it. I recognized it straightaway. It was a golden poison frog, one of the most toxic animals on Earth and rarely seen in the wild because it only inhabited one specific area in Colombia.

I'd read about these miniscule frogs at Oxford. They were fascinating creatures. Due to its coloration, I was sure this one was the phyllobates terribilis, the most lethal of the genus. Its poison was an extremely potent alkaloid neurotoxin that worked by paralyzing nerve impulses to the brain, resulting in cardiac arrest within minutes. Indigenous hunters dipped the tips of their blow darts in it to kill monkeys and other prey. Just one milligram could kill ten to twenty humans.

"Doctora!" The guards couldn't see me. I waved my hand at them, and they turned back to their chatting.

To my dismay, their shout and my movement had frightened the frog away. I marked the spot with a stick and carried on with my search for ruda. Eventually I found it, but no other frog. As I wended my way back to camp, I memorized the path I'd taken, then it occurred to me that if the frog was indeed P. terribilis, then I knew exactly where I was. I thought back to what I had read of it. If my memory was accurate, its habitat was a remote area of southwest Colombia near a river that flowed into the Pacific Ocean. The camp, then, was likely on a tributary of that waterway, which made perfect sense for a coca lab. They could bring in raw leaves from inland Colombia by river or even sea, and then ship out the finished product by the same route. I took immediate comfort in knowing my location, albeit approximate. I didn't feel quite so lost.

That evening, I brewed a strong tisane with the ruda and gave it to Frida, along with instructions for when the contractions and bleeding commenced and to come back if she was worried. Two days later she popped her head in the door and gave me a thumbs-up. She asked if she could get something to repay the favor.

"Jam," I said. "Any kind."

The following day, I told my guards that I needed to go out scavenging again, hoping to catch another glimpse of the P. terribilis. I had no particular purpose other than simple observation of a rare species that scientists rarely got to observe in its natural habitat. Once in the jungle, I pulled on my latex gloves in case of accidental contact and started my search. I soon found one. As I watched the frog, I realized it might be of use.

I had a large matchbox in my sack, a gift from the camp's cook who hadn't realized a few matches were left in it. I'd emptied them out to use the box on my foraging excursions, thinking it would come in handy for something. I had just such the use for it now. I slid off the lid slowly and quietly. Approaching the frog from the rear, I placed the palm of my hand under the leaf it was sitting on and quickly clamped the box over it. Even with the gloves, it was a delicate operation. The frogs sweated the poison, batrachotoxin, from their backs as a defense mechanism when they were stressed. The slightest brush of it on my skin was an irreversible death sentence.

Back at the infirmary, I went to work. Sliding the matchbox cover a crack open, I pressed a stick on the frog's back to activate the poison glands just under the skin. After a few seconds, milky beads peppered its torso. Using an eye dropper, I sucked up the poison and deposited it into the glass bottle. I did this until the bottle was full, then I released the frog in the jungle.

Having that poison in my possession changed my entire perspective on my captivity. It not only gave me power, but hope, hope that I could escape this dismal situation. I had no idea how, but at least now I had a secret weapon at my disposal. I'd also finally remembered the name of the river in the region where I reckoned the camp was located, the Saija, and thus another tiny piece of the puzzle snapped into place.

Days later, Frida turned up at the infirmary and extracted a small pot of strawberry jam hidden in her trousers. It was manna from heaven. I made it last as long as I could by rationing myself to a scant teaspoonful in the evening. I slid the jam off the spoon onto my tongue and let the sweet flavor leech onto my tastebuds as I shut my eyes to better savor every drop. During the day, if sadness caught me, I twisted off the lid, placed the jar over my nose and inhaled fully. Like Proust and his madeleines, the scent and taste transported me to a time of innocence when happiness was a Victoria sponge cake oozing cream and sticky jam or a thick slab of bread slathered with golden country butter and rich red preserves. When I finally finished off the jam, after eking it out at the end, I didn't wash the pot so I could preserve its aroma.

Weeks flowed by like the inexorable current of jungle rivers.

Early one morning a patient arrived by litter from an inland camp, and from across the room, I instructed the stretcher's bearers to put him in an empty bed. When I examined the patient a few minutes later, I started. It was a young woman, and judging by her civilian clothing, light complexion, fair hair, and blue eyes, a foreigner. I didn't let on that I'd noticed, but questions as to who she was and how she came to be here immediately pinged my brain. I'd have to wait. This was a place where the knowledge of anything other than how to manipulate an assault weapon was not encouraged.

She was in a dreadful state. Her skin was stretched over her cheekbones, her hair lank with sweat. But she was awake. She looked at me with large, vacant eyes. I spoke to her in Spanish. When she gazed at me blankly, I tried English.

"Can you tell me what your symptoms are? When they started?"

No reply.

"She doesn't respond, doctora," one of her minders said. They were so helpful.

"What's wrong with her?"

"A fever," the minder said.

He was really articulate, this one. I lifted her shirt and saw islands of white on an ocean of red skin. Dengue, an advanced stage, which would explain her stupor. Dengue shock. It did not augur well.

"When did she get sick?"

"I don't know."

"You can go now. Leave her with me."

The guard hesitated, debating whether he had to obey me, I supposed. I helped him decide by fluttering my hand in a shooing motion. He left.

I turned back to her. I doubted the FALC brought her here out of the goodness of their very black hearts. More likely, she was a hostage and keeping her alive was in their financial interest. Like myself, she'd fallen victim to fortune's fickle nature.

There wasn't much to be done for dengue. One had to let it run its course. And if it was the hemorrhagic kind, which I suspected was the case at hand, there was nothing to be done. Years ago, there'd been an outbreak at the village next to my camp. Four children, who were more susceptible to it than adults, had died. I gave my patient some purified water, supporting the back of her head so she could drink, then sponged her down with cool water. When I pulled off her trousers, my heart dropped. Traces of blood. The gastrointestinal hemorrhage would worsen.

I gave her every coagulant I knew of, but it was no match for the ravaging virus. She lasted four days. During lucid periods, she told me her name was Heather and that she was from Canada. Her story emerged in bits and pieces, mainly in the evenings when I had less to do and the night guard took frequent smoke breaks, which I insisted he do outside. She'd been backpacking solo through Latin America, starting the journey three months ago in northern Mexico.

When she was abducted by the FALC, she'd been staying with a family, whom she'd met in a town where they'd been selling eggs and vegetables in the market. They'd invited her to return with them to their small farm in the countryside, so their children could learn some English. She accepted. It would be a welcome respite from the road and a chance to see rural Colombian life. She'd been there six days when the FALC marched into the home just after midnight one night. They seemed to know she was there. The family said and did nothing when they seized her.

"The wife wouldn't look me in the eye, and I'd got really friendly with her," she said. "I think they set me up. I'd wanted to leave two days prior, but they insisted I stay for a few more days."

The FALC took her to a camp, where a week later she took ill after a trek through the rainforest.

She was weakening with the loss of blood. I sent a message to Omar, requesting that he send her to hospital, but he refused. A random backpacker, she was a low-value hostage, unlike corporate employees like oil workers or politicians. All I had was anger. I felt utterly useless.

"I'm not getting better, am I?" Heather said on her penultimate day on the planet.

I'd always believed in being frank with people about things like this, but now I found myself without the courage necessary for the truth.

"It takes time and a bit of luck." I rubbed her hand, then I had to get up quickly and close myself in my little storeroom so she wouldn't see me cry.

She kept asking me about a journal. Her captors had allowed her to pack a rucksack of clothing and she sneaked in a diary she'd been keeping of her travel adventure. "My home address is in it. Please contact my parents and tell them what happened to me. I haven't been in touch with them since I left. Tell them that I . . . I forgive them." She clutched my sleeve.

I asked her for the address since I assumed the journal was lost by now. All I could get out of her was "Sudbury."

Tears ambushed me once again and I rushed off. That night, I woke up in the wee hours with a sense of disquiet. I rushed to Heather's side and placed my fingers on her neck. It was still.

The guerrillas buried her in the forest. Her death crushed me. I'd had other patients die, but none had hit me so hard. I suppose it was because I saw myself in Heather. She had not chosen to be here, only died because she had been unfairly taken as a hostage, whereas guerrillas signed up for armed conflict and knew death was a possible outcome. Heather shouldn't have had to pay with her life for being a curious wanderer.

Why did wrongdoers win all the time? Why were they allowed to wreak havoc on innocent lives? And furthermore, get off scot-free? I thought back to my mother, empowered by instilling fear in me. Clifford Peever, enlisting abettors in his quest for superiority. Neither had got away with their acts of selfish violence. I'd seen to that. But now I was in the most powerless of situations, an imprisoned hostage. No one knew where I was, just like Heather, or even cared, with the possible exception of Carlota. I had isolated myself too much in my life. When I died, no one would remember me. It took me several weeks to shake the nimbus cloud of depression that had descended upon me.

Two months later, or perhaps it was three or even more — time had adopted a Brigadoon-esque quality — Frida showed up at the infirmary just before dusk, when I was due to be locked in for the night. She flashed me a hard look and said in an overloud voice, obviously for the guard's benefit, that she'd been having migraines.

"I can give you something for that. Come in."

Once she was seated inside, I stood in front of her, my back to the guard, palpating her forehead and neck.

"You're going to be transferred to a hostage camp in the interior," she said in a low voice.

The news jarred me. "What? When?"

"Soon. In a few days maybe. A squadron is coming in and they're going to take you back with them. I overheard Omar talking on the radio."

"But why?"

"Do you know la Comandante de Frente Tania?"

The name jogged something in my memory, then it came to me. Tania was the woman who had "bought" me from the highwaymen. She must've risen through the ranks fast. She was now Omar's superior. He was just a company comandante.

"She was here the other day and saw you coming in from the jungle. She asked what you were still doing here, and someone told her that you were in charge of the infirmary and what happened with the coca paste. Omar had told the superiors that the explosion had ruined the batch of paste and that they had to take a worker to hospital. He never mentioned you or using the coca paste on the boy. Tania's always wanted to put one of her allies at this camp, so this was her excuse to get rid of Omar. Word is that he's going to be transferred to a coca camp. The Army's doing a crop eradication operation, so as soon as they've finished we're moving back in to replant."

"How do you know this?"

"Omar told me. He wants me to transfer with him, but I don't know. It's really far. Listen, there's a boat coming tonight. You should try to get on it. Give me something so it looks good with the guard outside." Frida glanced at the door as she held out her hand.

"Thanks."

"I owe you for helping me. A lot of us owe you."

I felt warm with sentiment and patted her shoulder, but I hadn't time to dwell on it. I grabbed one of the empty sachets I made from folded palm leaves to hold remedies and pressed it into her hand as I considered what going to another camp meant. I'd lose my medic "privileges." I'd have to share close quarters with other hostages. Utter idleness. I'd been told what those hostage camps were like.

"If that doesn't cure your headaches in a couple days, come back," I said in a normal voice.

After I closed the surgery, I lay down to have a think. I had only a couple of hours to formulate a plan before the boat arrived.

The camp quietened as night deepened. I packed my rucksack, and when I heard the chug of the boat engine, I shrugged it onto my shoulders and waited. Two guards walked the perimeter at all times, crossing each other twice like hands of a clock. At night, I could hear them a little way beyond the rear wall of the infirmary hut, where they'd often stop and chat for a bit before resuming their paces.

I finally heard the buzz of voices. I had to time this well as my window for action was brief. I pulled on the surgical gloves, took out a safety pin that a guerrilla had given me and the vial of frog poison. I returned to the wall and listened. The guards were still talking. If I called out now, both would probably arrive. I didn't think I could handle both at once. The guards were still chin-wagging. Finally, footsteps. He was approaching.

"Compañero, I need your help. Es urgente," I called through the wall.

"¿Qué pasa?"

"A patient is having convulsions. I need you to hold him down whilst I get the medicine into him. I can't do it myself." My heart thudded. "Por favor. He's going to die if I don't get the medicine into him fast."

He hesitated, then said, "Ya voy."

I exhaled. I dipped the tip of the safety pin in the eyedropper vial full of poison, screwed the lid back on, and positioned myself flat against the wall next to the door as I heard the padlock click.

The door swung open. As he entered, I lunged behind him and swung my arm with the safety pin into the side of his neck. He grunted as he felt the prick and flung me back. I hit the floor. But I got him. He staggered then collapsed. Unfortunately, he was going to be sacrificed. I pulled out the safety pin from his neck and dropped it into the jam pot, which I'd washed for the occasion. After closing the lid tightly, I inserted it into a pocket of the rucksack. I raced outside, then paused in a shadow of a hut to listen for any sign that I'd been overheard. Silence.

A gibbous moon was shining that night, bathing the camp in a slight glow. In the murky darkness of the jungle, any light was bright, so I kept to the leeward sides of the huts to reach the kitchen area, which was on the opposite side of camp from the boat landing. I reached into my pocket for my matchbox and struck one of the few matches I had. I raised the tiny flame to lick the dried palm roof, hoping it would take. It whooshed with the new fuel. I sprinted to the rear of Omar's hut and waited.

The crackle of the flames eating the roof and the billowing smoke soon woke people. Someone shouted, "¡Incendio!" Fire! Guerrillas rushed out of their huts and started tossing water on the burning roof. Omar bolted out of his hut shirtless, shouting for water to be thrown on the roofs of the nearby huts so they wouldn't catch alight. I wheeled around the corner into his hut, going directly for the room on the side of his office.

My intuition had been right.

A barrel sat against the wall, a crowbar lying on top of it. I pried off the lid. It was filled with Colombian pesos and American dollars contained in plastic bags. I dug my hand in and shoveled the bundles into my knapsack until it was full. I slung it onto my back and poked my head out of the bedroom. All clear. I crossed the office to jump out the back window. Passing his desk, I stopped and pulled open his righthand drawer. Would my passport still be there?

I spotted a something that looked like a passport and papers. I heard a noise from the front door of the hut, scooped up the lot and jumped out of the rear window, landing in a heap.

Picking myself up, I stuffed the papers into the knapsack and folded myself into a crouch. I dashed into the jungle fringe around the camp. Keeping to the foliage, I made my way to the river. The boat's gangway was down ready for cargo, but I saw no one. The crew could be at the fire. I ran to the gangway and was halfway up when I heard a low growl behind me. I turned, my heart hiccupping. A man emerged from the brush holding a box. In the moonlight, I saw it was Ezekiel, the coca lab worker, holding a cage with an animal. We both stood paralyzed by our mutual discovery.

"Doctora, don't worry," he said in a loud whisper and walked onto the gangway. I had no choice but to move swiftly on to the boat.

He placed the cage on the deck and lifted a trap door. I recognized its prisoner, a margay, a fairly rare jungle cat whose leopard-like spots made it a prize for hunters. Anger rose in me, but I was in no position to assert this animal's rights.

"Doctora, you can hide in here." I caught a whiff of sooty air. The engine room. "The boat will reach Puerto Saija in the morning. From there, you can get a bus."

"Gracias." I lowered myself into the hold.

He jumped down after me. The height of the hold came to his waist. He reached out and pulled the cage into the hold, nestling it between the engine block and the hull so it wouldn't move. Frightened, the margay hissed.

"Suerte," he said then climbed out and closed the trap door, plunging the cat and myself into darkness.

I ensconced myself in a corner farthest from the engine and leaned my head back against the hull, taking deep breaths to let the adrenaline drain out of my system. A while later, I heard voices, the scrape of the gangplank being drawn in. The engine sputtered to life. The boat was moving.

I had done it. I'd escaped. I lowered my forehead onto my knees. But I wasn't free yet. My next challenge would be exiting the boat unnoticed and then getting out of Puerto Saija. The FALC likely had operatives in the town, and, as a pale-faced foreigner, I'd be easy to single out. All I knew about this area was that it was remote and poor. Its mostly Black inhabitants, descendants of slaves brought by the Spanish to labor on sugar plantations, suffered from long-term government neglect, which made them a prime target for money dangled by the FALC or narcotraffickers.

I stared at my companion, the margay, who was pacing around the cage, rubbing its body against the bars. It had been abducted from its home by a more powerful force, just as I had been, just as Heather, just as the forebears of Puerto Saija's residents. It struck me that I deserved it. I'd been that powerful force, too. Basically, I'd been just as awful as the guerrillas who had abducted me. I mercilessly milked the phyllobates terribilis for its venom, imprisoned the phoneutria fera and done the same thing. No living creature should be kidnapped from its home, sequestered in cages, tanks or padlocked huts. The margay seemed to finally accept its fate and sat gazing at me. The poor thing.

I soon had a raging thirst and a queasy stomach from the motion of the boat and the foul air. I wondered how much longer the trip was. Not long afterwards, the engine downshifted and then cut out. I heard shouts. We were arriving.

After the boat stopped, the trap door opened. Fresh air and light burst in. Lanky bare legs appeared over the lip of the trap door and a young man jumped into the space. I drew back as far as I could hoping to melt into the shadows. I needn't have worried. He only had eyes for the margay. He checked that it was still alive, then heaved himself up on deck.

"The cat is fine, but it stinks of shit down there," he called. "You want me to bring it up?"

"Leave it there until after we eat. We'll come back for it and take it to the client."

He left the trapdoor open.

The crew's voices and footsteps eventually faded. I waited about a minute longer, but the only noise was the lapping of the tide against the hull. I peeked out of the trap door. Nothing on deck. Then I poked my head out. All clear. I was about to pull myself out, then I remembered the margay.

I went back, picked up the cage and heaved it onto the deck and myself after it. Grabbing it, I walked down the gangway onto the shore. I saw a patch of trees. I jogged over and opened the cage door. The margay hesitated then realized what it was being offered. It bounded out and vanished into the brush. I hoped it would find some sort of home. I turned and walked quickly into town. It was daybreak, but people were already bustling about. I'd be noticed.

I spotted a taxi driver who was dropping off passengers a little further down the road and ran to catch up with him. "Bus station please," I said, huffing, as I closed the door a little too hard out of relief. I felt safer enclosed in this mobile tin can than on the street.

The driver kept glancing at me in the rearview mirror, likely curious as to who I was and what I was doing in this remote town. I averted my eyes. I didn't want to engage in conversation. Luckily, his mobile rang, forcing his attention away from me.

It was a brief trip to the station. I surveyed the row of ticket windows of various bus lines. One said it serviced Cali. It was the only destination I recognized, and it was a major city. I sped over and bought a passage for the next departure. As the woman counted out my change, I saw a calendar on the wall with dates crossed off. Today was the eighteenth of March. I had been in captivity nineteen months.

The bus was leaving as soon as it filled up. The woman at the ticket counter assured me that the morning buses to Cali sold out quickly and it would depart soon. It was a four-hour journey, she told me. I bought provisions from vendors ambling about the terminal — water, crisps, chocolate, biscuits, things I hadn't eaten in years, as well as a cup of black coffee that a woman was selling from a thermos, a baseball cap, and a newspaper.

I boarded the bus, choosing an aisle seat so I wouldn't be easily seen through the window and pulled the hat low over my eyes. By now Omar would have discovered my escape and figured out that I'd made my getaway on the boat and would likely be in Puerto Saija. He would've radioed ahead for lookouts. The first place they'd check was the bus station, but I didn't have a choice. If I stayed in the town any longer, someone would dob me in. Just as that thought raced across my mind, I noticed a young man in the bus yard, hands in his pockets, pivoting as his eyes scoured the terminal. I opened the newspaper and held it in front of me like a shield, my heart thumping. All he had to do was go to the ticket windows and ask if anyone had sold a fare to a foreign woman, and I'd be done.

A steady stream of people boarded my bus. Someone wanted access to the window seat next to me. I moved aside and peeped out of the window. The suspected spy stood at a ticket booth, two windows down from my bus line. The driver hefted himself behind the wheel and started the engine. I looked around the bus. We were almost full. Did he have to wait until every single seat was taken? My skin grew clammy.

The man reached my bus line's window, conferred with the woman, then his head jerked around to look at my bus and he pointed. She nodded. The driver turned on loud salsa music and lurched into gear, keeping the door open in case of late arrivals. The man ran after the bus, yelling and waving his arms, as we rolled out of the terminal. The driver didn't hear him over the music and kept going. We were on a side street. Then the bus braked to turn onto a highway and came to a full stop to wait for a gap in the riverine flow of morning traffic.

Thumps sounded from the side of the bus. The man was right under my window, then, just as the driver let up the brake to merge and the bus moved ahead, the man jumped onto the bottom step of the doorway. At the same time, the driver punched the accelerator and the bus jackrabbited forward to squeeze into a lane. The spy lost his handhold and tipped backwards into the roadway. Several people called out, but the driver, absorbed in his music and focused on the traffic, didn't hear. He pressed a button and closed the door. I twisted in my seat to check the spy. He was picking himself up, growing smaller as the bus gained speed.

The passenger next to me shook his head as if to say, "What an awful driver." I settled back into my seat and took deep breaths to calm myself. Thanks to pure luck, I was on my way, but now the FALC knew where I was headed, which created another obstacle, exiting the Cali bus terminal. They'd undoubtedly have a welcoming party there for me, as well. I considered getting off a stop sooner, but they'd probably have lookouts at all the bus stations, and they'd be small towns where I'd stand out. I was better off getting off at Cali, which would have a biggish bus station. Still, I'd have to do my best to dissipate into the crowd.

Once in Cali, I could get to Bogotá, where it would be easier to hide for a few days whilst I considered my next move. Flying to the capital city, I decided, might be a safer option than taking a bus. As far as I knew, the FALC hadn't mastered air-jackings. I had no idea what I was going to do after Bogotá. I had to get out of Colombia as fast as possible, but where to? I told myself I had money and time to decide and relaxed.

I remembered I had my passport and took it out of my knapsack. At seeing a corner of the dark blue cover, I felt the sink of disappointment. UK passports were red. I turned to the front. Canada. I opened it to the identification page. A familiar face stared dully back at me. Heather McKenzie.

It made sense that her passport was on top. Mine was probably in the back of Omar's drawer. The lack of a passport was another obstacle I'd have to hurdle, but I'd deal with it later. I stuffed it back in my rucksack and picked up the newspaper, which I'd dropped to watch the chase. It was always a bizarre feeling, coming out of the jungle and seeing the vertiginous swirl of events happening in a world that I had no participation in or even knowledge of. Something like a pupa emerging from a cocoon. I turned a page, and a headline caught my eye.

Spider Venom Startup Takes on Big Pharma.

Every muscle in my body tightened. I read on, scarcely able to breathe. It was a story from Miami.

Since its introduction nine months ago, an inexpensive supplement made from South American spider venom has taken the market for erectile dysfunction drugs by storm, decimating sales of pharmaceutical brands.

"We are able to produce a highly effective product that works on both men and women at an affordable price," said Miami-based entrepreneur Guy Westerphal, president and CEO of SelvaPharma, which manufactures the supplement called Neutria. "Big Pharma has only themselves to blame."

SelvaPharma can barely keep up with the soaring demand for Neutria, which is produced from the venom from the Brazilian wandering spider or phoneutria fera, found in the Amazon jungle. 'We're now getting orders from Europe and China. We're expanding our

manufacturing operation to twenty-four/seven so we can keep up,'
Westerphal said.

Westerphal said he was not worried about competition as the
patented formula for Neutria was developed from his own research in
the Venezuelan jungle.

His own research. I felt nauseous. I forced myself to read on.

"Big pharmaceutical companies have tried to harness the
crucial element in the venom but were never able to do it successfully.
It was a painstaking process that took years so I doubt anyone can
replicate it easily," he said. "All the work has paid off spectacularly as I
knew it would."

The active ingredient of the supplement lies in the spider's
venom, which is known to cause painful, long-lasting erections when
men are bitten.

Guy Westerphal's wife, Ellie Westerphal, said that her husband
became obsessed with the idea of making the venom for human
consumption.

I thought I was going to be sick. Ellie Westerphal. The estranged
wife?

"There were moments where I doubted his sanity, especially
when he went to live in the remote jungle, but I trusted his instincts,"
she said with a laugh. "Besides, once Guy gets an idea in his head,
there's no talking him out of it."

Especially when he went to live in the jungle? No wonder he'd been
so vague whenever I'd asked him about his wife. Guy was still very much
married to her, no doubt communicating with her from the internet café
several times a week. He'd slipped that one time, mentioning her name
and said it was his assistant in Miami.

I felt the thunderclap of incontrovertible truth in my head. He hadn't
loved me at all. I was merely a convenience that he'd availed himself of.
He'd used my emotional attachment to strengthen the tenuous cobweb he
had spun to snare me. He was the spider, and I the fly. The irony was rich.
I laughed to the point of hysteria, and then had to stifle myself when I
noticed my neighbor looking askance at me.

Guy had sucked me in, chewed me up and spit me out. The only
promise he'd kept was to make a fortune out of Neutria, a fortune that he
hadn't wanted to share. I supposed it was too easy to shove me out of his
way. I wondered if his wife knew about his relationship with me, had

tolerated it because of the wealth it would bring them. What about his daughter? Had he made that up too, knowing somehow that I'd have a soft spot for fathers and daughters?

I felt that hard chip of anger re-emerge and lodge itself in my core. Cold, bitter anger. I realized that it had never gone away. Perhaps it never would.

When the bus arrived at the Cali station, I sat up alert and looked out the window. My eyes rested on two men lolling conspicuously against the wall where the bus pulled in. Spies? I positioned my hat low over my forehead as I filed down the aisle to the door. I bowed my head and plunged into the crowd clamoring to retrieve luggage from the hold. I glanced back and saw one of the men striding toward the bus. Feeling a surge of panic, I looked around for an escape route. Then I noticed the coach had one of those luggage compartments that opened on both flanks of the vehicle. I dove into the compartment and crawled through to the other side, shoving boxes and bags out of my way and behind me, hoping that they'd shield me from view. I exited on the other side of the compartment, which a porter was unloading, then walked quickly to the entrance where the buses arrived, instead of passing through the terminal, and slipped out onto the street.

I hailed a taxi about a minute later and told the driver to take me to the best hotel in the city. One of Guy's legacies. He'd shown me that a good hotel was worth it, and I had money.

Once installed in a fifth-story room at the Intercontinental, I bolted myself inside and crumpled onto the bed. Just thirty-six hours ago, I was a hostage in a jungle camp run by psychopaths with a future as an imprisoned slave. Now I was lying on soft, clean sheets with a bath, television and a refrigerator at my disposal and the future yawned so large, it was paralyzing.

My brain, my senses, my sinews, were all overloaded. I couldn't cope with anything right then. I plunged into heavy slumber and slept through to the next morning. When I awoke, I ordered bacon and eggs, toast, and lashings of jam for breakfast, which felt lavish indeed, and turned on the TV to an all-news channel. Famines in Africa, bombs in the Middle East, right-wing rallies in Europe and America. It was remarkable how little the world ever changed. There was nothing about Guy or Neutria. He'd even kept my name for the supplement. I thought back to what he'd told me early on. He'd turned out to be as he advertised, a predator who played according to the "law of the jungle." And I'd thought he was joking.

I now had to decide what to do. Borneo beckoned. I'd gone on a study trip there whilst at Oxford and had almost directed my research efforts there, but then I ran across the Amazon's phoneutria fera and became intrigued.

I went downstairs and made use of a computer with internet access in the business lounge to look up travel routes to get to Samarinda in the Indonesian part of the island of Borneo. As I was doing so, the sharp edge of the chip kept poking me.

Guy.

Should I let him get away with this? I considered. If I got my rightful half of the Neutria money, I could open my bio station, perhaps in another country in the Amazon basin or somewhere else such as Borneo. I could still fulfill my dream. Plus, seeing his face when I turned up and demanded my half of the business would be amusing, to say the least. He'd offer to pay me off straight away. To Guy, money was the solution to everything. I could take the cash, open my rainforest conservancy after all. I changed my destination to Miami and found direct flights departed daily from Cali.

I sat back in the chair. How was I going to do this? I didn't actually want to go to British authorities and report my passport stolen. One of my mother's fellow folk medicine practitioners had voiced suspicion to the weekly newspaper after I found Mum dead, a vial of crushed hemlock that had been mislabeled as one of her mixtures, "Bilberry/gingko biloba," next to the kettle. The mug lay on the floor next to her amidst the puddle of its spilt contents. "Adelaide had worked with herbal remedies her entire life without mishap. I don't think she would've made such a mistake," Tillie Pink had told the local rag. But a recent vision examination had found that poor old Mum had the beginning of cataracts in her left eye, which was precisely why she'd been consuming a bilberry/gingko infusion. Her death was ruled "by misadventure," but Tillie had continued pestering the police for a criminal inquiry even after the inquest until she finally dropped her crusade. So no, I did not want to raise my head above ground to have it lopped off.

Heather's passport. The hotel clerk hadn't raised so much as an eyebrow when I'd provided it to register, nor at the cash payment. As I'd found out long ago, all gringos looked much the same to locals in Latin America. But immigration officials were a different matter altogether.

I returned to my room and leafed through the passport. It had a Colombian entry stamp of three months ago. Good. Then I studied Heather's photo, obviously taken when she'd enjoyed rude health. She had long chestnut brown hair that extended well past her shoulders. Mine brushed to my shoulders, the longest it had ever been, and was now prematurely striped with grey, thanks to the rigors of captivity. Hair color was an easy fix. Her face didn't resemble mine but was rather average with no noticeable characteristics. I could wear glasses when I went up to the booth. That would help. She had brown eyes, as opposed to my green. One could get contact lenses of different colors, I thought. She was also thirty, as opposed to my now forty-four. How adept were immigration officers at determining age?

At any rate, I needed a new wardrobe. Badly. After nineteen months of wearing my same khaki trousers and shirt, hand washing them repeatedly, they were holed and fraying. They also hung baggily on my now coat hanger-like frame. I'd always been lean, but now I was positively gaunt.

After asking the concierge for directions to the nearest shops, I set out. At a boutique, I asked a young saleswoman what people her age wore these days, and bought "skinny" jeans, something called a crop top, a bright pink rhinestone-trimmed baseball cap, and high-topped sneakers. I looked completely foolish and unlike me. I was on the verge of ripping everything off me then I realized that was exactly what I was seeking.

I decided to embrace my new persona. I wore the outfit out of the shop, shoving my jungle togs into a rubbish bin at the corner. I bought more clothing at several other boutiques then I finished at a salon where I had my hair dyed to match Heather's.

"You could use a trim. Did you cut your hair yourself?" the woman said looking into the mirror in front of me and holding out my shaggy locks.

"I'm letting it grow at the moment. I want long hair."

"You don't have to wait. I can put extensions on you."

By my expression, she knew I had no idea what she was referring to. She buzzed off and returned holding a long sash of hair. I smiled with comprehension. "Absolutely perfect."

The next day, I found an optometrist and bought brown contact lenses and glasses with plain lenses. He was surprised at my request.

"It's rare I get someone who wants brown lenses," he said. "Everyone wants blue or green."

"We all want what we don't have," I said light-heartedly, buoyed by how well my plan was working out.

As I walked back to my hotel, I noticed a beauty spa that advertised "Rejuvenation Treatments!" in its front window along with before and after photos of a woman's profile. The after photo was indeed much younger looking. I entered to inquire and wound up getting injections of botulism, of all things, around my face.

"Your face will swell for a day or two, but when it goes down, you'll see a huge difference," the woman said, handing me an ice pack.

Back at the hotel, I gazed at a different woman in the mirror. Yes, I could do this. I would go to Miami.

I wasn't going to be able to travel with a bag of cash. I emptied out my rucksack on my bed to count the money and then I found the other papers I'd taken from Omar's desk and forgotten about. Among various papers was a diary of sorts. On the inside cover, a hand scrawled note in Spanish and English said, "If found, please return to Ed and Eleanor McKenzie," followed by an address in Sudbury, Ontario. I propped a pillow behind me and settled against the bed's headboard to read it.

It turned out Heather had done a runner from a drug rehabilitation place that her parents had forced her into. Her first night out, she picked up a guy at a bar, stole his money and jewellery and hit the road south, surviving by employing the same modus operandi along the way. She was an able writer and I read the whole journal of confession and adventure in one go.

Night had fallen. Outside the window the mountainside was dotted with pricks of light that disguised the slums as a twinkling fairyland. Nothing, I thought, was ever what it seemed on the surface.

I resumed counting the money, and found I was in possession of the rather tidy sum of forty-seven thousand dollars. The following day, I opened a bank account and made sure that I'd be able to withdraw money in the United States. Then I went to the post office and posted Heather's journal to her parents along with an anonymous note stating the circumstances of her death and how she had personally helped me. As I left the post office, I felt content. I hadn't been able to save Heather's life, but perhaps I'd done something to preserve her memory.

After booking a flight for four days hence, I bought a suitcase and researched Canadian accents online, rehearsing a few words distinguishable from standard American pronunciation. However, I spent most of the time in my hotel room allowing my eyes to acclimate to the lenses and my facial puffiness to retrocede, as well as watching television to hone my accent and vocabulary. After several days, and without close scrutiny, I looked reasonably like Heather McKenzie.

On the day of my flight, though, I was inevitably nervous. Colombian passport control would be the first test of my disguise. The immigration officer barely looked at me or my passport, stamping it and handing it back in one fluid motion. The bigger test, I knew, would be entering the United States.

Several flights had arrived at once in Miami so there was a huge queue in the airport immigration hall. Customs officers with dogs trotted up and down the lines of people, sniffing their luggage.

As the queue inched up to passport control, I stepped out to see how closely the immigration officer was inspecting passengers. My stomach lurched. He was holding up passports to compare faces against photos. Panicking, I left the queue and after going to the ladies' room to splash water on my face to get a grip on myself, I joined another queue, again scrutinizing the officer to see how closely she was examining photos. I felt hot, as if running a temperature, and I was sweating profusely. I noticed a uniformed officer holding a lead on an Alsatian and watching me.

I had to maintain my composure, or they could think I was a drug mule. I still had my vial of batrachotoxin in my cosmetics bag. In Cali, I'd sealed the top well with tape and wrapped it in plastic to prevent leakage. It wasn't illegal, but still, if they searched and opened it and got so much as a drop on their skin, they'd be in seizures within minutes, and I'd be in handcuffs.

I went to the ladies again. I stayed in the toilet for what seemed like an eternity, but it was probably only five minutes. I splashed water over my face and arms, drew a couple deep breaths and walked out. As soon as I joined a queue, the officer with the Alsatian approached. My heart banged against my ribcage, then I scoffed at myself. Dogs were trained to detect specific substances. It was impossible that batrachotoxin would be on the list.

The officer walked the dog around me in a circle twice, but the dog gave no sign of detecting anything untoward. Wordlessly, the officer moved on to another passenger. I had passed that small test, but obviously I couldn't change queues again. I kicked myself for being so bloody stupid.

My heartbeat pulsed in my ears as I neared the counter. When it was my turn, I forced a smile at the officer. He looked up at me.

"What's the reason for your trip?"

"Visiting friends."

"Remove your glasses, please."

I slid the glasses off. Beads of perspiration rolled down my sides from my underarms. I should never have attempted this. It was foolhardy. I was going to be caught and then what? I hadn't really considered that possibility.

His eyebrows puckered in a slight frown as he examined the passport. Then the drug dog barked. Everyone turned towards the direction of the noise, including myself and the officer. He stamped my passport and handed it back, still peering in that direction.

"Welcome to the United States."

PART IV

I lodged at a tawdry motor inn in a busy commercial area near the airport. With a stained carpet and scratched furniture, it was quite a step down from the Intercon in Cali, but it suited my needs for keeping a low profile and conserving funds.

After settling in, I headed straight to an ancient computer for guest use in the lobby and soon located SelvaPharma's address on the company website, as well as loads of articles about the new wonder supplement, Neutria. People were raving about it, saying it had ramped up their sex lives, saved their marriages, made them feel decades younger. It was just as successful as Guy had predicted, and all based on my research. I couldn't help but feel a blush of pride over my fury at his theft and betrayal.

Guy certainly wasn't press shy. One article in the Miami Herald quoted him as saying he was getting offers from venture capitalists and investors all over the world, and he was considering listing the company on the New York Stock Exchange. It sounded like Guy's typical bluster.

No one seemed to question his claim to the research that had led to this spectacular triumph, except one person. Buried deep in the pages of my search results, I found a column in a pharmaceutical trade journal from several months prior by a Dr. Ahmad Abdelaziz.

Neutria Needs More Scrutiny

While the supplement Neutria has proven overwhelmingly popular, more attention needs to be paid to the science behind it. I personally studied the P. fera venom some years ago. Isolating the Tx2-6 element, which causes priapic reactions in some men, but not all, is a complex chemical process. Furthermore, muting its hazardous effects requires even more advanced biochemicals knowledge and skills. It would have taken quite a bit of time and experimentation that my company, as well as others, were not willing to invest. As far as I know Mr. Westerphal has no background in advanced science. He's a businessman, and a smart one to be sure, but I'm scratching my head as to exactly where he gained this formula and how it was tested. Mr. Westerphal has been notably vague in his public statements about the origins of Neutria. To paraphrase Shakespeare, methinks something smells rotten in Denmark.

I had made Tx2-6 work, precisely because I, unlike corporate researchers, was not bound by time and money. I sat back in my chair, feeling somewhat vindicated that at least one person was questioning Guy's claims.

Research achieved, I needed to find Guy. I made friends with the Paraguayan desk clerk, a young man named Pablo, by speaking Spanish, which he greatly appreciated since he was still learning English. I asked him about taxis and public transport.

"Taxis are very expensive here and buses are terrible. You should hire a car," he said.

After I explained that I'd been living in the Amazon jungle for two decades and hadn't had a driving license in years, he spotted a business opportunity and offered to rent me his battered white Corolla. "You know how to drive, right?"

It'd been a while, but yes. Before I turned away, I decided to test just how popular Neutria was.

"Have you ever heard of a supplement made from spider venom?"

"Neutria? Who hasn't? I haven't used it myself, but my friends have. They say it makes their girlfriends wild. Why?"

"I think I ran into the researcher in the jungle a few years ago."

"That guy must be a gazillionaire for sure," Pablo said.

The hype was real, then.

Armed with Pablo's directions, my first trip was to a shopping center. My driving skills were rusty to say the least. Trying to ignore toots and dirty looks from other motorists, I jerked along the road, stamping on the accelerator and brake too hard, but I arrived, perspiring but without mishap. I bought a cheap mobile phone, a thick notepad and pens, sunglasses, magazines and newspapers, energy bars, apples, orange juice, yogurt and cheese, as well as a small cooler bin with a reusable ice pack, and a pair of binoculars. I also purchased a loose, long skirt and a bed pan, and a stack of coloring books for adults, along with felt pens, crayons and colored pencils. I found a quiet residential area off the main road and drove around for a while to practice. The hang of smoothly accelerating and braking gradually returned.

The next morning, I sallied forth at seven o'clock and headed for the office park in west Miami where SelvaPharma was headquartered. It was called The Cascades, which turned out to a misnomer since there was no cascade that I could find. The misrepresentation, however, made it quite fitting as the location of a business run by Guy Westerphal.

I recognized him as soon as the electric blue sports coupe bounced into the car park. He wheeled into the space with a sign reading "Reserved SelvaPharma CEO" and braked to an abrupt stop. Music blared for an instant before the engine turned off.

He got out of the car with a jaunty step and a leather briefcase. I must admit, Guy Westerphal millionaire executive looked far more the part than Guy Westerphal jungle researcher. He was clean shaven with a fashionable haircut that feathered his hair back at the sides, wearing a suit coat with casual trousers and no tie.

He walked up the cement path, opened a glass door and was swallowed by the sterile brick building where SelvaPharma was headquartered. I took a deep breath. I'd done it. Located Guy. This was the easy part.

The hard part, which I hadn't at all anticipated, was the actual impact of seeing him again. My legs jellified. My stomach somersaulted. My mouth filled with dust.

It had been almost two years since I'd last laid eyes on him. I was surprised at how strongly I reacted. I put it down to shock at seeing him, but after I calmed down, I realized I was afraid of him. If I confronted him and asked him for my rightful share of the company, he could trump up some charge to have me thrown in prison again, claim I was some charlatan out to extort him although I could recite the Tx2-6 formula and other facts from memory. But that wouldn't be enough. Guy could simply state that wasn't the correct formula without revealing his. He had the money to hire a private detective, find out about my using a false passport, that I was wanted in Venezuela, have me clamped in irons and deported. I suddenly felt a panicked urge to forget about Neutria and instead drive to the airport and board a plane to somewhere far from Guy.

I pushed back the impulse. I couldn't let him get away with this. It was my life's work that he'd stolen. My life's work! And he'd done it in the most despicable, underhanded way possible — by exploiting my heart and my dreams.

"No," I said aloud. "No, no, no, no! NO!" I banged the steering wheel with the flat of my fist with the final utterance and rallied myself. You have to stand up for yourself against bullies, against unfairness, like you've always done, Rowena. You can't let them win! Once more unto the breach, dear friends! Stiffen the sinews, summon up the blood.

I picked up my pad and pen and jotted down his arrival time and the car's number plate. Then I steeled myself to get out and take a closer look. As I peered in the window, any doubt that it was Guy was immediately dispelled. A book, "All You Need to Know about Terrarium Arachnids," lay on the passenger seat. One of the articles I'd read about him said he had a warehouse full of Brazilian wandering spiders and displayed a photo of him beaming as he posed next to a glass tank.

I returned to the Toyota and settled in for a long day, picking up a pretentious magazine I'd bought the day before, Haute Miami. Suddenly, Guy's face beamed at me from a glossy page. He was everywhere! He was pictured standing in front of a mansion arm in arm with an attractive, dark-haired woman. My heart clutched. The headline read:

At Home with Guy and Ellie Westerphal

The short article described the couple as "philanthropists and devoted patrons of Miami's arts scene," noting that Ellie Westerphal sat on the Miami Ballet's board of directors, whilst Guy Westerphal had recently donated money for the "Westerphal Tropical Medicine Center" at the University of Miami School of Medicine.

How lovely. Really, how very, very generous of Mr. and Mrs. Guy Westerphal.

I perused the photos of their opulent spread in the exotic-sounding "Cocoplum Estates." The back garden of the seven-bedroom home fronted Biscayne Bay and two jet skis, bearing the names "Phoneutria" and "Fera" on their hulls (very slick, Guy!), were tethered to a small jetty. There was an inviting aqua swimming pool and a grand fireplace in the lounge, de rigueur for Miami's Arctic winters, naturally. The house was decorated with extravagant sprays of orchids, the blooms matched the color scheme in each room. It was all gorgeous and oh so perfect. My miserable huts and hammocks and outhouse were risible by comparison. No mention of his daughter. Had she, too, been by design?

I flipped another page and found, as if by divine punch in the gut, my answer. A picture of a girl sitting at a benchtop in the kitchen, textbooks open in front of her, pen poised in hand.

The Westerphals' fourteen-year-old daughter Elspeth wants to study biochemistry and follow in her father's footsteps to bring more Amazon plant remedies to the world.

The girl had traces of both Guy and Ellie in her face. I'd never had even a speck of a chance with Guy, and he'd known that all along. He'd manipulated me completely, a puppet master pulling the strings of his marionette. How he and Ellie must have chortled about ugly, stupid, misfit Rowena on his calls from the internet café.

I flung the paper instrument of my torture through the window. I knew then what I wanted from Guy. It wasn't money. Money had never mattered much to me, and I had forty-plus thousand dollars. Not much, I supposed, in the scheme of things, but enough. No, I wanted to ruin him, humiliate him, expose this purported pillar of the community as nothing more than the mountebank that he was.

I felt the impulse to do something, take some sort of action. I got out and retrieved the magazine from where it had landed next to a Mercedes and ripped the pages about Guy to shreds. Then I sprinkled the pieces over the bonnet of Guy's Jag. Confetti for the great hero. A childish move, but nonetheless satisfying.

Just after midday, I was busy coloring a mandala when Guy exited the building. I sat up, eager to gauge his reaction to his littered car. He stopped short, studied the mess for half a second, then simply got in the Jag and drove off. The shreds flew off his car and fluttered in the wind like real confetti. The arrogance of it.

Tossing the coloring book into the back seat, I pulled out behind him. He drove for about fifteen minutes into a place named Coral Gables and turned into the horseshoe driveway of a peach-colored building with a golf green behind it. I drew up to the curb and observed through the binoculars. Young men clad in collared shirts matching the color of the building and bright white Bermuda shorts rushed out from the front portico to open Guy's car door. He jogged up the steps and entered. A well-polished brass plate on the wall next to the door stated "Hotel Strada" in elegant script. A valet drove off in his car, returning minutes later with the keys in his hand. A business lunch meeting, perhaps. Guy certainly liked dining at hotels. I felt a painful stab as I remembered how happy I'd been at those meals in the Puerto Ayacucho hotel where he'd dazzled me with the potential for our partnership.

About an hour and a half later, Guy emerged and handed something to the valet, who jogged off. Through the binoculars, I noted his carefully coiffed hair was rumpled and he was tucking his shirttails into his trousers. He had done more than lunch at the hotel. The evidence that he was a chronic philanderer, that I was likely one of many, was at once both comforting and hurtful. But I had no time to parse sentiment. Guy roared out of the driveway. I followed. By his route, I soon gathered he wasn't going back to The Cascades.

He turned into an industrial park full of warehouses — with loading docks and lorries hauling containers — and stopped in front of the entrance to a warehouse. There was no sign indicating what was inside, but I assumed it must be where he kept the spiders. He disappeared inside, then after half an hour or so, he exited and drove back to the office. Just before six, he exited and drove to a residential area with a gate and guardhouse, Cocoplum Estates. Guy entered through a lane marked for residents, the gate arm raising automatically, and he sped through. Another lane for visitors led by the guardhouse where a uniformed woman checked every car against a clipboard. A surveillance camera was positioned on the roof of the guard hut. I couldn't risk it. I drove by, looping around the estate hoping to find a service road that would perhaps be less policed, but there was no other entrance.

I returned to the motor inn, pleased with my day's work. I'd learnt quite a bit about my quarry.

I followed Guy on and off over the following ten days to establish his daily pattern. It wasn't hard. Humans are creatures of habit. I minimized the chances of being recognized by buying various styles and colors of wigs and other accessories such as hats and sunglasses. I couldn't do much about the car, but a white Toyota Corolla was about as nondescript as you could get. I even went into the SelvaPharma office one afternoon under the pretense of seeking a different corporate tenant whose name I'd lifted from the building directory in the main entrance. As I stood in SelvaPharma's foyer stuffed with jungly-looking plants, I felt a thrill at being so close to Guy, yet his having no clue.

He went a few times a week to the Hotel Strada at lunchtime and once a week in the evening. I never saw his paramour until one day I decided not to tail him but wait instead to see if I could spot her. Ten minutes after he left, I was rewarded with the sight of a willowy woman, fashionably dressed in a tight skirt and heels, with a waterfall of blondish hair down her back, coming out alone. Everyone else had exited in twos or threes. It was a good possibility that she was Guy's lover. I confirmed it at Guy's next lunch by again waiting after he left. Sure enough, exactly ten minutes later, the same woman came out. I followed her to a real estate office in an area called Coconut Grove. I parked and walked by, stopping to pretend to look at properties listed for sale in the window. She was sitting at a desk, so I assumed she worked there.

I bought a vanilla ice cream cone and strolled around Coconut Grove. It was a lovely little shopping district with a marina full of yachts and boats. Under a sky filled with clouds like massive puffs of whipped cream, I sat on a bench in a grassy waterfront park and looked at the map on my phone to see how far it was back to the motel. I noticed that my location was across from Cocoplum, which was marked on a promontory jutting into the sea just south of me. I looked up at the piece of land within view. Perhaps I could find Guy's house from the sea. The magazine article had described the back garden as fronting the bay.

I'd just passed a sign on a pier that said, "Bicycles and Kayaks for Rent," so after scarfing down the rest of my ice cream, I retraced my steps to the wooden hut. After confirming from the over bronzed attendant that what I'd been looking at was, in fact, Cocoplum, I hired a kayak.

As I paddled, I relaxed as I fell into the rhythm of oar-in, oar-out. The Atlantic Ocean was a rippled sheet of blue-green glass. Seagulls wheeled and cawed. Thickets of tangled mangrove roots bunched along the shoreline, tiny birds hopping amongst them. I felt my balance restored as I took my place as simply another element in the ecosystem. It didn't last long enough. The mangroves soon gave way to a row of palatial mansions and various types of boats and other aquatic toys. Cocoplum.

It was harder to find Guy's house than I thought. Cocoplum wound around several canals, likely manmade in order to charge top prices for "waterfront property." I paddled up and down the waterways, pausing every now and then to drift past workers cleaning pools, plucking weeds and mowing grass as I gave my aching arms a rest. Finally, I came upon the moored jet skis "Phoneutria" and "Fera." I stopped and stared at the ornate Italianate mansion. It looked even grander than the magazine pictures. I recalled what Guy had told me when we first met, about his mother promising him they would live in a palace. I was sure that the manor in front of me boasted chandeliers galore and a frozen meat locker stocked with ice cream. His beleaguered mother had engrained in him the belief that he was entitled to a palace, no matter who or what he had to trample to get it, because he and his mother had been denied their due. Of course, his childhood tale of woe could've been falsehood, but I thought it was probably one of the few true things he'd told me.

One of the French doors opened onto the terrace beyond the pool, unleashing two girls in swimming costumes. A dark-haired woman followed them holding a book. The kids raced to the pool and jumped in with great splashes. One I recognized as Elspeth, the daughter. The other was darker skinned. A schoolmate, perhaps. They tossed a ball around, clambered onto giant inflatable swans and splashed about, shrieking and giggling. Ellie sat in a poolside chaise-longue and opened the paperback in her lap. The protective mother hen.

As I watched the scene of domestic bliss, a tide of envy mixed with sadness swept through me. I longed to be that woman in the chaise-longue. Be a mother, a wife, have a family, a normal life. Ellie looked up from her book and scolded the children for jumping into the shallow end. She turned and caught me observing them. I remained still as our eyes fused. I wanted her to see me, to make myself known in some way, although of course she would have no idea who I was. She broke her gaze and returned to reading. After another few moments, I picked up my paddle and propelled myself forward.

When I returned to my hotel, I drew the curtains across the window that overlooked the car park, hung the "Do Not Disturb sign" on the doorknob and sank into bed. The images of Ellie and the girl scraped my insides. Mother. Father. Daughter. The picture-perfect family. Something I never had in childhood and never would in adulthood. Why had I denied my own desire for such happiness?

I couldn't get up the next day or the next. I dismissed the maids. My life had no purpose. I was nothing more than a piece of human furniture whose purpose was to be used by others. It had been a mistake to come to Miami, to seek Guy. I should've stayed with the guerrillas where I hardly ever thought of him, where I was needed. It hadn't been so bad.

On the third day of my hibernation, there was a hard rap at the door. It was Pablo come to ask if I needed the car after his days off. It had turned into a good sideline for him.

"No, thank you," I called through the door.

"Are you sick? Can I get you something?"

I didn't want him hovering and fussing, or even worse, barging in, so I forced myself to get up and open the door. "Just sleeping in. I've had bad insomnia lately."

"Well, let me know if you need anything." He turned and I went to close the door, but then he pivoted. "By the way, that supplement Neutria you were asking me about? Someone died from it, and now there's a big investigation. Thought you might like to know. It's been all over the news the past few days."

I thanked him and shut the door. Dead? Investigation? The news galvanized me. I grabbed some clothes from the floor, threw them on and six minutes later I was reading a front-page story in the Miami Herald on the lobby computer.

Complaints surface about venom wonder supplement

Federal authorities are investigating Neutria, the libido-boosting supplement derived from spider venom, after numerous complaints from users that it causes cardiac arrythmia, including one case that resulted in death.

The Federal Trade Commission is looking into about 350 complaints that include elevated blood pressure, loss of feeling in extremities, respiratory issues with repeated use and an investigation following the death of a 58-year-old man in Boston.

"This is a blatant attempt by BigPharma to drive SelvaPharma out of business," said Guy Westerphal, CEO of SelvaPharma, the Miami company that manufactures the supplement. "Neutria was tested extensively before it was launched on the market and was found to be safe."

Westerphal downplayed Neutria's adverse effects, saying 350 complaints are a tiny fraction of the nearly half billion pills that have been sold worldwide since Neutria was launched. "Everything you ingest has side effects," he said.

He refused to reveal details about how, when, and where the supplement was tested. "All that is proprietary information that I can't reveal, as much as I would like to. Pharmaceutical companies are dying to get their hands on it because Neutria has blown their overpriced drugs out of the market," he said.

News of the investigation has renewed questions in the pharmaceutical industry about how Westerphal developed Neutria since he has no background in any scientific field. He has repeatedly said the supplement was based on his own research in the South American jungle.

"I've been scratching my head since Neutria appeared," said Dr. Ahmad Abdelaziz, a professor of pharmaceutical science at New York University. "This just isn't something you come up with overnight. Westerphal's a brilliant marketer, I'll give him that, but his coming up with this supplement is hard to believe. Now that accounts of serious side effects are surfacing, including a possible death, he owes the public an explanation."

Westerphal had a short response. "I owe nothing to anyone," he said. "I'm sure that an autopsy of this poor man will reveal underlying health conditions that caused his death."

Westerphal has been linked to shady dealings in the past. In 2002, he testified against his former boss and colleagues in an insider trading scam at a hedge fund where he worked. Westerphal was the only one who was not charged. Five years ago, a gold-coin trading scheme that he ran was the target of an investigation by the New Jersey Office of the Attorney General. The operation was shut down, but no charges were filed.

A Herald investigation also found that Westerphal was never

enrolled in the prestigious universities that he claimed to have degrees from. Spokespeople for Boston University and the University of Pennsylvania said they had no record of Guy Westerphal ever attending either university.

The furor over Neutria underscores another problem: the lack of regulation over dietary supplements.

The article continued, but there was nothing more about Guy. So, he was a crook who kept getting away with his crimes. Not surprising. But maybe he wouldn't this time. At last, a crack had appeared in his fortress-thick wall. I could take advantage of this.

I looked at the name of the journalist who wrote the article: Chloe Quinn. I'd seen her name on other stories about Neutria, as well. I picked up the phone and rang the Miami Herald, then I told Pablo I'd be needing the car after all.

I met Chloe Quinn at a restaurant called Versailles, improbably, since it served Cuban food and everyone was speaking Spanish.

She smiled when I made this observation. "This is the heart of Little Havana," she said. "I have no idea why it's called Versailles. It's pronounced the Spanish way — 'Ver-SIGH-es'."

We ordered Cuban coffees and pasteles de guayaba, guava-filled pastries. I felt a twinge of nostalgia. "It reminds me of Venezuela."

"You said on the phone that you met Guy Westerphal there."

Nodding, I focused my attention back on her. She was somewhere in the indistinguishable period of twenties and thirties, and already had her notepad and pen beside her right hand on the table. A good sign.

Over the next hour, I gave her a broad outline of what had happened with Guy. She listened intently, scribbling in her notepad, and interjecting several times to clarify the sequence of events or other facts. A couple times, she held up her hand and I paused, waiting for her written words to catch up to my spoken ones.

I also didn't go into the details of being held hostage, merely saying that I'd been in a remote area of Colombia until I happened on a newspaper article about Neutria.

"That's a hell of a story," she said when I finished.

"I realize it may sound improbable but it's the truth."

"I believe you and so will many others. Everybody in the pharmaceutical industry has been wondering about Westerphal, but nobody wants to go on the record with their doubts."

"Except Dr. Abdelaziz."

"Yes, except him." She tapped her pen on her chin. "Don't take this the wrong way, but do you have any proof of what you've told me? Even a photo of you and Guy? I believe you, but that's the first thing my editors are going to ask."

I shrugged. "I have nothing. Guy took everything from me. I left the camp with just the clothes I was wearing." It occurred to me that I couldn't even prove I was Rowena Aldus since I was using a false passport.

"I'll do some checking around and get back to you. It'll take a few days. Are you talking to any other media, by the way?"

"No. I thought you'd be the ideal candidate."

"Great." She insisted on paying my share of the bill and as we walked out, she pressed her business card into my hand. "Call if you think of anything else. My mobile's on there."

Driving back to the motel, I wondered if I'd done the right thing. She seemed sympathetic, but her response didn't sound all that promising. Still, I felt better. Someone now knew the truth, someone who had power. I resumed my surveillance of Guy. His daily schedule hadn't altered.

The next day, I was startled by my phone ringing as I sat in the car outside the Hotel Strada during one of Guy's midday trysts, looking up at the windows and wondering which one was his room. I'd given the number to just two people, Chloe Quinn and Pablo. Pablo never phoned me. I felt a burst of hope as I answered.

"I've done some backgrounding," Chloe said. "I hate to say it, but I didn't turn up anything that corroborates your story."

A weight dropped on my shoulders. I hadn't realized how much I'd been counting on this journalist.

"I found your articles on the phoneutria fera, however, and I located Professor Medford-Jones. Did you know he died five months ago?"

"No," I said in a dull voice.

"I also called our stringer in Caracas. She checked with the National Guard and British Embassy. Rowena Aldus died two years ago while in custody in San Carlos de Rio Negro. Cause of death unknown."

The weight got heavier. The comandante must've faked my death to absolve himself of blame for my escape. It would be well-nigh impossible to unravel that without going to England for my birth certificate and other legal documents. For all intents and purposes, Rowena Aldus no longer existed. I didn't even look like her with my disguise.

"I did contact a few other people in the biochemistry department at Oxford. I found another professor who remembered you, Philippa

Stockley. She said that you were, quote, 'a rather strange, mousy little thing. Very odd, not quite all there, in my opinion.' End quote."

Philippa Stockley was a cunt, but I didn't say that. I did my best to keep the rising emotion out of my voice although I didn't entirely succeed. "Philippa Stockley was jealous of my close relationship with Professor Medford-Jones. They'd had a fling years before and he'd ended it. She never quite got over it."

"Unless you can give me something concrete to back up your story, my editors say we have to can the article. I have an idea, though."

"Yes?"

"You could file a lawsuit against Westerphal. People make all kinds of charges in lawsuits without having evidence. We write about them all the time."

It was worthy of consideration. "Where do I find a lawyer?"

"I know one who might be willing to take your case. I've dealt with him a number of times. He plays hardball. And you wouldn't have to pay him. He takes a cut of any settlement as payment."

I took down the name and phone number of one Hugo Santiago. After I hung up with Chloe, I called it. His assistant perked when I said that I had the "true story behind Neutria" and made an appointment for the following day in the late afternoon.

The law firm of Santiago & Sanabria was located on the twenty-seventh story of an office tower, one of many in the manmade forest huddling Miami's flashy Brickell Avenue. The lift sped toward the sky, leaving my stomach somewhere near the ground floor.

His office boasted a panoramic view of Biscayne Bay, spangled under late sunshine and daubed with the white of yacht sails. The place was decorated with memorabilia of pre-Castro Cuba. Flags, photos, posters, even a street sign and an impressive display of old cigar box art on a wall. The man himself was older, sixties, I guessed, spiffily dressed with a matching burgundy silk handkerchief and tie, a gold tie pin and matching cufflinks. The greying strands of his remaining hair were swept back from his forehead and fixed with some sort of glistening hair varnish.

In accented English, he offered me a seat and my choice of coffee or water. I accepted the latter, and an assistant soon returned with an espresso for him and water for me.

"I have to confess that I was intrigued by your call," he began, raising a leg so its ankle rested on the other knee. "Guy Westerphal and Neutria. Not the real deal, I take it."

"Not at all." I launched into my story, telling it much the same way as I told Chloe Quinn, although this time I added the detail of our romance.

From time to time, he stretched his arm, flashing his gold cufflinks, to write on a lined yellow pad with a fountain pen, of all things.

"IP theft," he said slowly as he looked over his notes when I'd finished.

Hearing my story boiled down to that label made it seem rather paltry, but it was accurate enough. He looked up, put down his pen and clasped his hands across his stomach. "We need to prove you had the IP before Westerphal arrived on the scene."

Basically what the journalist said. "I have nothing. I had to flee the country in the middle of the night."

"We need something or Westerphal could have the case thrown out as a nuisance suit. You mentioned an article you wrote. I can have my assistant locate that. What about research permits? Can you get copies from Venezuela?"

I felt a slash of vexation. I'd told him I was persona non grata there. On top of that, I recalled suddenly that the last permit actually had Guy's name on it. "Possibly."

"If you can get any evidence, documents, emails and so forth, come back and we'll see if we can get legal action going. Right now, there's nothing. You could also file a complaint with Federal Trade Commission and let them do the investigating." He stood. "Thanks for coming in."

I was being sloughed off. On the way out, I requested to use the "restroom." When I came out, the assistant and Santiago were talking in his office with the door slightly ajar. I paused in the hallway.

"It sounds like scorned lover revenge. She had an affair with Westerphal and she's sore he broke it off and struck it rich," Santiago said. I shouldn't have told him about the romance. I hadn't thought how it would come across to others. I was a bloody fool!

"Pretty wild story, though," the assistant said. "Like something out of a movie."

"And I thought I'd heard them all," the lawyer said.

He didn't believe me, and I wasn't naïve enough to think Chloe Quinn really believed me either. I slunk out of the office and battled my way back to the motel through heavy traffic, feeling the crunch of defeat.

As I inched along the Dolphin Expressway, it occurred to me that I had one last card to play. Ellie. I could confront her and tell her about Guy's and my affair in the Amazon, about his current affair, for that matter. It wasn't nearly as strong as I would've liked, but it would create problems for him, although I suspected not many. If he was a chronic adulterer, she probably knew and accepted it as the tradeoff for the money.

By the time I reached the motor inn, I had abandoned the idea. How would I get past security at Cocoplum? There wasn't even anywhere to park outside the entrance to lie in wait for her, and even if I did, the guard would probably notice. I could kayak my way to their back garden, run through and ring the front doorbell. But then how would I get out of Cocoplum? If she rang security or the police, I'd be trapped. The small reward wasn't worth the risk.

That night, as I watched the news for anything about Neutria, I decided it was time to leave Miami, go to Borneo and forget about Guy. I'd accomplished nothing, but at least he was under investigation. Still, the fact that he'd got away with ruining my life chafed me. Bullies always won. Before the news was over, I drifted into a sour sleep.

In the wee hours, I awoke with a new decision clear in my head. I did have another card up my sleeve. It was drastic, but I'd come all this way. I wasn't going to let it be in vain. And Guy deserved it.

The following day I surveilled Guy as usual. It was a Thursday, the day of his evening rendezvous at the Hotel Strada. Close to six, he left and drove to the hotel, gave a cheery wave to the valets as he handed them his car keys and entered through the door that a doorman pulled open for him. He usually took about an hour and a half, so I waited about an hour, working on more pages in the coloring book, before leaving my car parked on the curb and entering the hotel. The place was abuzz with people. A sign on an easel gave the reason: "Welcome to the Tropical Medicine Society of Latin America Annual Conference."

I took a seat in the lounge with a good view of the lift and ordered a scotch, neat. As I waited, my ears caught the staccato rhythm of Spanish being spoken at the various tables. I recognized Venezuelan and Colombian accents, as well as the singsong inflections of Argentina and other more neutral accents I couldn't quite place. Close my eyes and I was back in South America.

Right on time, the lift doors hissed open, and he stepped out. I leapt to my feet. "Guy!" I called.

His head twisted as if I'd yanked it on a string. The initial look on his face was fright at being recognized. Then he squinted, trying to place me. I looked quite different to when he'd known me. My hair was long and dark, and I had on the clear glasses I'd bought in Cali and my sunhat. I removed both as I grabbed my scotch and maneuvered myself in front of him.

"Fancy running into you here, of all places," I said.

He froze with realization. "Rowena?"

I felt a boost of power at having pushed the ever-so-smooth Guy Westerphal off balance. "This is incredible, meeting you like this," I said.

He looked around wildly to check if anyone was observing our encounter.

"How about a drink?" I said.

"I really have to . . ."

"One drink. You owe me that surely. No hard feelings on my part, I assure you."

His Adam's apple bobbed. "Sure, why not?" He was making an effort to sound jovial, but to my satisfaction it rang false.

We entered the lounge where a bow-tied pianist had started playing show tunes. Guy steered us to a pair of chairs in a quiet corner, which suited my purposes exactly. A mini-skirted waitress flitted over. He ordered a single-malt scotch, neat, as I knew he would. Habits rarely change.

"This is quite a surprise," Guy said after she'd left. "I thought you were . . . never mind."

"Dead? In prison? The thing is, Guy, you overestimated the power of your money. It doesn't buy you loyalty. That goes to the highest bidder. Gosh, you've gone quite pale. Have my drink while you wait for yours. I haven't touched it yet." Using two fingers, I pushed the tumbler across the small round table. "As soon as I saw you walk out of the lift, I recognized that strut. I said to myself, 'That must be him.' The last time I saw you, you were in khakis and a sweat-stained hat, with a bushy beard and hair down to your collar, and much thinner. But now you're a corporate executive in a designer suit. Neutria. You kept my name. You did say it was perfect."

Guy gulped the scotch in one swallow. "Listen, Rowena, the comandante told me you were dead. I had no idea you were still alive. It was chaotic that day. I want to make it up to you."

I wasn't interested in hearing his excuses. "Do you really think I'm going to fall for your promises again, Guy? You planned the whole thing. I've had plenty of time to think it all through over the past couple of years."

Perspiration broke out on his forehead. He loosened his tie, unbuttoned the collar. I was enjoying his discomfort enormously. "How much do you want?" he said.

"The problem is it wasn't only my research you stole. It was my life's mission and my dream, a future for the indigenous communities in the Amazon. And, this will sound terribly trite but it's true, it was my heart. How do you put a price on all that?"

"I made an inexcusable mistake, but I didn't know . . . I'm really sorry. I don't know what else to say."

The waitress delivered his scotch. He grabbed it and downed it in one gulp.

I leaned forward and stared into his eyes. "Stop the bullshit, Guy. I know it's hard for you, but for once in your life, stop the dissembling. I'm not the gullible, lonely Rowena anymore."

"It was for my daughter. My wife was going to leave me and take Elspeth to Europe. I'd never be able to see her. You wouldn't want a little girl growing up without her dad, would you?" His eyes implored me for sympathy. "I couldn't let that happen. You understand, don't you, you of all people? I had to prove to my family that I could be a success."

"There would've been plenty of money to go round, but you had to prove that you weren't like your father, and it didn't matter how you did it," I said, realizing that Ellie was just as much Guy's victim as I was. "Ellie doesn't know any of it, does she? She thinks you legitimately bought or licensed the research. She quite rightly doesn't want to be married to a swindler, a two-bit charlatan."

"Listen, we can still do the community development project. I'll finance it, you run it. We'll set up model sustainable villages like we talked about, clinics, food production, potable water systems. Tell me what you need. Blank check. We can still do it."

"I was quite envious when I saw your waterfront mansion in Cocoplum, and Ellie and Elspeth." The pure shock on his face gave me the most satisfaction I think I'd ever had in my life. Then he seemed to recover, his eyes wide with realization.

"It was you. In the canoe. Ellie told me some creepy woman was staring at her. We thought it was one of those crazy animal rights people."

"And the torn magazine pages on your car. Do you remember that?" I checked my watch. It was taking longer to act than usual.

"Jesus, how long have you been . . .?"

A convulsion struck him midsentence. I smiled. He looked horrified as he realized what was happening. The muscles in his limbs contracted into another seizure and he keeled onto the floor, wheezing. I knelt next to him, smoothing his hair. For just a flash, we were back in our sex shack. He clutched my forearm, his eyes pleading with me for help, but even if I'd wanted to, I couldn't. There was no going back with batrachotoxin.

"Law of the jungle, Guy darling," I said. "That's what you told me, is it not?"

The waitress tottered over and gasped. "Oh my god!"

"Call an ambulance!" I ordered.

Even if medics arrived quickly, they wouldn't be able to do anything. She pattered off, clucking like a decapitated hen.

A couple of people flew to his side. The scene was starting to get attention, so I backed out of the scrum and slipped out of the lounge. I estimated he had about five minutes. Between convulsions, his neural synapses would spasm as their signals died one by one, and his lungs would labor increasingly under the gradual paralysis.

I strode smartly out of the hotel, got in the Corolla and drove to the airport, where I parked, leaving the keys and parking ticket in the car. After I checked in for my flight to Jakarta, I texted Pablo and told him where to find it then stamped on the phone in the bathroom and chucked the pieces into the bin, along with the vial of batrachotoxin that I had in my pocket as I joined the security queue. I never wanted to see poison again.

When I felt the wheels lifting from the ground, I pressed my head back into the seat. I would now have to start over again. Funny how patterns repeat in life.

PART V

Three months later:

Jungle towns are much the same everywhere in the world. Dirty, boisterous, a little primitive, often on a river. Samarinda, the capital of Indonesian Borneo, kept to the description except it boasted a grand mosque, its dome and minarets imbuing it with a classic silhouette at sunset. Five times a day the muezzin summoned the devout to prayer with a robotic-sounding incantation.

I set myself up as Heather McKenzie in a small furnished flat and found a woman who spoke decent English, Annisa, to tutor me in Bahasa. I learnt languages easily and quite enjoyed them as an intellectual exercise. I also welcomed her company and her instruction about local culture and customs. I had the hair extensions removed and the brown color lopped off. I was back to my short cut, which was much cooler and easier to manage in the high humidity. I took out the brown contact lenses but kept them in case I needed them. I concentrated on keeping busy, attending cultural exhibitions, touring local parks and waterfalls, strolling around markets.

But I kept thinking of Guy. I regretted murdering him, leaving his little girl without a father. In a perverse way, I'd repeated my own past. What if Ellie Westerphal was abusive like Adelaide Aldus? What, then, did I accomplish with his death? A momentary feeling of power and victory? I realized with a start that revenge, perhaps, was just as selfish as the act that spawned it.

The novelty of my new surroundings soon wore off, and I felt despair born of lack of purpose looming around the corner. I wondered if I should head back to South America, to another country in the Amazon basin. I emailed Carlota, letting her know I was alive and well. I mentioned that I was in Asia — keeping my whereabouts vague was a prudent course of action, I thought — but considering a return to South America. She replied that she was glad to hear from me but counselled me to remain at a distance. She said she'd forward on by email any correspondence that arrived.

"Two people from Caracas called me wanting to get in touch with you several weeks ago. They said they were from the Institute of Scientific Research and one from the British Embassy. When I asked how they got my name, they wouldn't say so that made me suspicious. I gave them the official line from la Guardia, that you died of a fever while in custody. I hope I did the right thing. Take good care of yourself."

I pondered who they could've been. The journalist in Miami had mentioned something about a reporter in Caracas. Would that reporter not have said who she was? Maybe she'd decided to pursue the story in the wake of Guy's death. It was too late now. She'd missed her chance.

After my daily lesson that evening, I was leaning on the railing of my balcony in the slight coolness that dusk brought and missing my camp.

It struck me that like the real Heather McKenzie, I'd used distance to escape my parents, but I actually hadn't escaped my mother at all. In fact, by killing her, I'd become her. By the very act of taking her life, I had subsumed hers. My years in the jungle, I saw, were penance for my subconscious guilt. Consciously, I'd convinced myself she deserved her untimely end. But I'd ended my own life in a way too. I'd become afraid of being around people in case my murderous side, the Adelaide Aldus I'd inherited by nature, nurture or both, would surface again. I chose toxic spiders as my companions because they had the capability to wound and kill as I had. The corporate scientists had, in fact, been right. I wouldn't have ever finished my research. I only completed it because of Guy. Then I killed him. And the guerrilla at the camp, although I suppose I could be legitimately excused from that one. They had taken me captive, after all. I had to fight back with whatever means I had to escape. Nevertheless, I'd allowed Adelaide to take over once again. I really was as despicable as she was.

But Rowena Aldus was dead. I suddenly understood that the comandante had given me a gift by killing off my previous self. I now had a new identity, a new landscape. I should look forwards not backwards. Not many get such a second chance.

As the last muezzin of the day echoed, I had a stroke of clarity. From this point on, I would study flora, not fauna. The truth was, I liked being a healer in the guerrilla camp. I enjoyed interacting with people, having them respect me, seeking my advice and expertise, more than I'd ever thought. That was the good side of my mother. I should emulate that.

The following day, I told Annisa of my new plan and asked if she knew of any healers who used traditional medicine. She said she'd make some inquiries. Three days later, she had the name of her daughter's husband's second cousin's brother-in-law who ran a small ecotourism lodge in the highland rainforest. One of the excursions they offered tourists was to a shaman in a nearby village. I was dismayed. That wasn't what I meant at all.

"I don't want a tourist show. I want to study the plants, academically."

She placed her cool hand on my forearm to reassure me. "Stanley said you should come and visit. There are a lot of people with that knowledge around there."

I wondered whether it was simply a ploy to get Stanley a well-paying foreign customer. Then again, I reconsidered, what harm was there if it was? It would be a bit of an adventure and a chance to get out of the city. I booked myself into Stanley's lodge for the following week.

As I kitted up for the trip over the next few days, buying sturdy boots, a rucksack and so forth, I noticed a short, squirrel-faced man turning up in my path. Leaning against a wall smoking a cigarette when I exited the flat in the morning. Peering in a shop window as I was walking out. Perusing magazines in the stationer's where I bought an English-language guidebook and maps. The next day, he sauntered into the café where I sat having a coffee and bun. Feeling a bit spooked, I gulped down my elevenses and headed straight home.

Was he following me? If he was, he wasn't doing a very good job. Perhaps he meant me to see him. A government official letting me know I was under surveillance? I thought of Heather McKenzie's passport. It was likely an imprisonable offense.

I told Annisa about the man. She thought it was probably an admirer. "We don't get too many foreigners here. Maybe he's working up the nerve to make your acquaintance. I'm sure it's nothing."

I put the man out of my mind since I was going to the lodge. Perhaps my absence would be enough to cause him to find another object for his admiration.

On the day of my departure, a Land Rover with the logo of Rainbow in the Rainforest Ecotourism Lodge on the door picked me up. A middle-aged Norwegian couple outfitted in new safari gear were already seated, and the back was loaded with boxes — supplies, I presumed. It would be a three-hour, uphill journey, our driver Agung, who was Stanley's son, informed us.

It was a rugged and at times slow ride, especially after the paved road ended, but I felt back in my element again, surrounded by nature. A peacefulness I hadn't felt in ages enveloped me. I knew I'd done the right thing by undertaking the expedition.

The lodge wasn't fancy, much like any jungle camp. We had plain but comfortable wooden cottages with mosquito nets over the beds and ate in a communal building, lots of tropical fruit, some chicken and fish invariably accompanied by rice.

Stanley, his wife Indah, and Agung ran the lodge. They introduced me to the local shaman, who frankly wasn't that receptive to having someone poking around and asking questions, which bore out my original assumption that his was a hocus-pocus act. I questioned Stanley further and found out there were female healers in villages farther from the camp. Women, I'd found, were less bound by ego and more readily shared their knowledge, especially after I told them I'd pay them. They didn't get much chance to make their own money. I settled into a routine of travelling every other day to a village, and on alternate days taking walks in the forest to find the plants I was learning about.

I delved into it with relish, and gradually, a new plan unfolded before me. I knew from my childhood that there were plenty of societies and organizations that financed research into natural medicine. I could try to obtain funding from them. I could even set up a traditional medicine camp to teach others about plants and also to heal. I spoke to Stanley about it one evening after dinner. His eyes sparked.

"That's a marvelous idea, Heather. You could base it out of here. We could work out an arrangement. You'd live here and offer classes in traditional medicine and plants in return for room and board a cut of the profits. It would be something else we could pitch to tourists, give us an edge over the competition. I like the idea of a healing center too. That could be a future development."

I wasn't keen to rush into anything since my previous attempts at business partnerships had resulted in disaster, so I said I'd have a think about it. But as I strolled back to my cottage, my heart leapt with the prospect of finding a niche in the world. There didn't seem to be much of a downside. If it didn't work out, I could simply pack up and leave. The following morning, I accepted Stanley's offer and said I'd return to Samarinda on Agung's next trip to pack up the flat and move into the lodge.

"Terrific!" Stanley clapped me on the shoulder. "I'm going to see if I can hunt a wild pig to celebrate tonight."

After breakfast, I prepared to head into the rainforest for my habitual walk. As I slung on the woven bag I'd bought from a village woman to use for collecting plant cuttings, I saw Indah getting a couple of cottages ready, which meant new arrivals were due later that morning. I was glad that their business was picking up.

It was a fruitful ramble that morning and I went farther than normal. I was finding all sorts of interesting plants and fauna, vividly colored butterflies and insects. I took photos and snapped off twigs and leaves. The world, it seemed, was casting its arms wide open to me. Around midday, I turned around and started wending my way back to camp. A few times, I heard movement in the forest and halted, statue-still, hoping to spot a larger mammal, a monkey perhaps, but there was nothing. A feeling of foreboding nibbled me, but I dismissed it and carried on. I spotted a column of ants on the ground near a bush, so I crouched to observe the tiny insects carrying bits of leaf far bigger than their bodies.

"Hello, Rowena."

My head whipped around. My name. My real name. Was I hearing things?

To my utter shock, Guy Westerphal was leaning on a tree trunk, holding a walking stick in both hands in front of him. He doffed his hat and pulled out a handkerchief, with which he wiped his sweat-soaked forehead and hair. He smiled, although it was more of a grimace. Only half his facial muscles appeared to work.

"This is getting to be a habit with us." His voice, coming out of one side of his mouth, was thick and sluggish.

I was too stupefied to speak. Was it really him? How on earth was he alive?

"You're probably wondering how I survived your murder attempt," he said, reading my mind. "A combination of my luck and your mistakes. The night you chose to poison me was right during a tropical medicine convention. After you left me for dead in the hotel, there were plenty of doctors in the lounge to perform CPR and keep me alive until the ambulance arrived.

"My heartbeat was faint, but it was there. The right side of my body was paralyzed. The doctors thought it was a stroke, as I did at first. The shock of seeing you, the stress I was under due to the FTC complaints and investigation into Neutria. But a few days later, a Colombian doctor, one of the ones who had rushed to my aid in the lounge, came by the hospital to see how I was.

"He asked me to describe the symptoms of the attack and then said he'd seen the whole thing. He said he didn't think it was a stroke at all. The convulsions sounded a lot like I'd ingested a neurotoxin. He'd seen similar cases in Colombia when he was practicing medicine in remote areas where indigenous tribes used poison-tipped blow darts to hunt animals but in those cases, death was almost certain within ten minutes. He thought it was very strange. I scoffed at his idea outwardly, but of course, it wasn't as far-fetched as I made it out to be. I knew at once you'd poisoned me with some type of obscure toxin, likely meaning to kill me. You were good, I'll give you that. I'd never figured you going that far.

"After I recovered somewhat, I told one of the Brazilian researchers who advised me on the spiders about my suspicion that I'd been poisoned with a neurotoxin. Like the Colombian doctor, he was puzzled. He said it should've killed me, but then he came back to me after doing some research. He said those poisons work best with intravenous administration, delivered by something like a blow dart. Also, if it had been mixed with strong alcohol, that may have weakened it significantly. He also said there was little research on how the toxicity levels held up over time,"

In my zeal for vengeance, I'd chosen the easiest method of administering the batrachotoxin, but not the most efficacious. And I'd only used several drops of it in case he detected the taste too early and spit it out. On top of all that, it had probably lost a lot of its potency. Stupid miscalculations on my part.

"Don't worry," Guy went on. "I never reported you to the police. It would have led to too many questions about Neutria. Instead, I hired a private investigator to find you. I figured you'd contact that lawyer in San Carlos at some point, so we got a hacker to monitor her email, and bingo, one day a message from you popped into her inbox. We traced the email's IP number to Samarinda, Borneo, which made perfect sense. I remembered you'd mentioned Borneo before, and when I discovered that Indonesia had no extradition treaty with the United States, I figured that's where you had to be. We had a local PI stake out the internet café. He soon located you and found out from a neighbor in your building that you were called 'Heather.' He sent me a photo. You're back to looking like your old self now. By the time I arrived in Samarinda, the PI said you'd left, but he found out from the neighbor where you'd gone. So here I am." He swept out an arm like a magician on a stage.

The man with a squirrelly face. Guy's operative, of course.

I found my voice. "So, you found me. Now what?"

He ignored my question. "SelvaPharma, FYI, is kaput. The government shut us down. Too many complaints."

"I told you it needed further trials."

He continued the soliloquy he'd come to give. "The money's basically all gone because of lawsuits and the divorce. I'm back at square one, only now with half a body, thanks to you."

He scratched his chin, covered in several days' worth of stubble. "You know, I didn't arrive in Venezuela with the plan to take your research, but you were just too easy of a mark to pass up. I had an investigator check you out the day before I met you. I knew you were living at a fleabag hotel and didn't have a goddamn penny to your name. Then you showed up at the restaurant stinking of cheap perfume, wearing makeup like a clown and in flip-flops. You saw Ellie in Miami. Did you really think I could fall in love with you? I mean, Ellie was above me in every way, but I won her. I wasn't going to slide back down the hill after fighting to get to the top of it." He laughed, which turned into a spluttering cough. I felt that hard chip of pure hatred at my antagonist punch through again. "Killing me, though, seemed a little harsh. I'd just had you arrested. The comandante told me you'd be in prison for a long time. But you got out of it. I underestimated you."

"Why are you here, Guy? What do you want? This is all in the past."

He gave a bitter chuckle. "Yeah, it's easy to say that when you're not half paralyzed. You quoted my line in the lounge that night. 'It's the law of the jungle, Guy, darling.' I heard you loud and clear. So now I'm saying it back to you, 'It's the law of the jungle, Rowena, darling'."

He whistled and the squirrelly man stepped into sight aiming a long gun at me. This was it, I thought. No matter how much we sought to untether the past, it remained moored forever within us, threatening to unleash itself and engulf the present at any moment. I was never going to escape the consequences of my past actions. I had to be content with the fact that fleeting happiness was my lot in life. At least, I'd had that. The truth of it, I was a "phoneutria fera," a savage murderess. I'd done enough damage. It far outweighed what little good I'd done. I didn't deserve to live any longer.

I held out my arms to the sides as if nailed to a cross. "Go ahead and tell him to shoot to kill then we'll both be free."

I stared at Guy. I was going to confront death with open eyes, in all senses of the phrase. I wanted to see it coming.

A pfft sound came from behind me. Something flashed through the air and pierced the gunman. Clutching his neck, he cried out, staggered forward and fell. Guy stared in astonishment. A second pfft. Something got him on the left side of the chest, right in the heart. How appropriate. He dropped.

Stanley emerged from the bushes holding his blow gun. He'd told me his darts were poisoned with sap from the upas tree, a cardio toxin. I bent over Guy as he struggled to breathe.

"It's tough, the law of the jungle, isn't it?"

Epilogue

Stanley and I dragged Guy and his nameless henchman deeper into the forest to the area where wild boar roamed, where Stanley had just come from. The pigs and other animals would devour the bodies. When Stanley and I returned three days later, we found only a few remnants of clothing and burnt them.

After that, Stanley reported the men as missing on a jungle walk that they'd insisted on taking themselves. The police wouldn't do much, he said. It was inhospitable terrain to search and if people were foolish enough to take off by themselves into dangerous territory, they assumed the risk. He was right. Nothing happened.

Of course, I couldn't tell Stanley the whole truth of Guy's vendetta against me. I didn't want to scare him off, and some things are better kept to oneself, but I did tell him a partial truth. That he was an old lover whose violence I'd escaped in Miami. He somehow traced my whereabouts and wanted to kill me.

"If he couldn't have me, no one could," I said.

Stanley sympathized. He'd known men like that. They existed everywhere.

I did indeed move to the lodge. Over time we established a healthy stream of guests coming to learn about plant and traditional medicines. Carlota even visited once. Stanley's family came to regard me as one of their own, akin to a maiden aunt, thus I achieved the familial setting and companionship I'd always lacked. I take as much delight in the grandchildren as their real grandparents. When the children were little, I spent hours coloring with them until they outgrew that activity, although I continue to do it to music when alone in my hut. I also introduced Indah to jam-making and we started making preserves of various tropical fruits to sell, although I still order my beloved marmalade from England which I never revisited. Eventually, we established a healing center, a version of the dream of the Amazon bio station that I'd once had, a better version, I think.

Two decades later, the passage of time and age has led to a nagging conscience. I have undertaken this exercise of writing the truth as both humble confession and therapeutic catharsis. The manuscript will remain locked in a box until my death.

I owe a strange debt of gratitude to Guy Westerphal. It was because of him that I found the other side of my mother in myself: the healer. Ultimately, that's what I hope you will remember of me, dear reader, Heather the healer, not Rowena the savage murderess.

About the Author

Christina Hoag is a former journalist who has had her laptop searched by Colombian guerrillas, phone tapped in Venezuela, was suspected of drug trafficking in Guyana, hid under a car to evade Guatemalan soldiers, and posed as a nun to get inside a Caracas jail. She has interviewed gang members, bank robbers, thieves and thugs in prisons, shantytowns and slums, not to forget billionaires and presidents, some of whom fall into the previous categories. Now she writes about such characters in her fiction.

Christina's noir crime novel *Skin of Tattoos* was a finalist for the Silver Falchion Award for suspense, while her YA novel *Girl on the Brink* was named one of Suspense Magazine's best for young adults. She also co-authored the nonfiction book, *Peace in the Hood: Working with Gang Members to End the Violence*, which is used as a textbook at University of California Los Angeles, University of Southern California and other academic institutions.

She has won several awards for her short stories and creative nonfiction essays, which have been published in anthologies and literary journals including *Shooter* (UK), *San Antonio Review, Santa Barbara Literary Journal,* and others.

She's a former staff writer for the *Miami Herald* and *Associated Press* and reported from 14 countries around Latin America for *Time, Business Week, New York Times, Financial Times, Sunday Times of London, Houston Chronicle*, and other news outlets. She is a graduate of Boston University.

Born in New Zealand, Christina grew up in seven countries. She now lives in California, where she has taught creative writing at a maximum-security prison and to at-risk teen girls. She is a regular speaker at women's conferences, writing conferences and organizations, book clubs and stores, and libraries.

Sign up for her newsletter at https://christinahoag.com.